TRAIL TO NOWHERE

When John Bristow, rangeboss to Alan Gardea, found Charley Schilling with a worn-out horse and a posse in hot pursuit, he did exactly as Alan's father had done for him, Bristow, many years before – he led him into an *arroyo* where they would be safe from pursuit; for a time.

But the posse was not to be so easily shaken off. Led by Sheriff Comstock, they were determined to get their man. But they had not reckoned with the local feeling in Wyoming; and they had reckoned, unwisely as it turned out, on the co-operation of the local sheriff; but he was a Wyoming man also.

'The best in the business.' *Kirkus Review*

TRAIL TO NOWHERE

JACK KETCHUM

ROBERT HALE · LONDON

First published in Great Britain 1991

ISBN 0 7090 4524 7

Robert Hale Limited
Clerkenwell House
Clerkenwell Green
London EC1R 0HT

Photoset in North Wales by
Derek Doyle & Associates, Mold, Clwyd.
Printed and bound in Great Britain by WBC Print Ltd,
and WBC Bookbinders Ltd, Bridgend, Glamorgan.

1 The Fugitive

It was autumn in Wyoming, which meant the nights were cold and before warmth appeared in the days it was close to afternoon.

Southward, into Colorado, with some of the most heart-stirring scenery on earth, the nights were cold but the days warmed up earlier and in fact most autumns there was genuine heat.

The farther a man rode, with his back to Wyoming, the less cold it got at night and the warmer the days were, until in northern New Mexico, east and west of Raton, the weather was about as ideal as it could be, and the same as what usually obtained elsewhere – bitter nights and chilly sunbright days in a virtual fairyland of massively panoramic scenery, with plentiful water and mountains like Fremont peak to inspire awe – the trade-off began. New Mexico, even the northern reaches, had a look of desert, with wind and sand and poisonous flying and crawling things that commonly inhabited deserts, although actually northern New Mexico was to some extent a continuation of southern Colorado, meaning it got more frequent rainfall than the more southern parts of the territory, and it had good grass and browse almost year around, the result of a more temperate pattern of weather.

Before the southerly desert began, some miles south of the Colorado line there was a stockman's paradise which ran east and west for many hundreds of miles. It was within this strip of warm, rarely genuinely cold country where grass flourished, there was little cause for winter feeding and there was adequate rainfall – the legacy of being close to Colorado – that those stockmen fortunate enough to have found this cowman's paradise had, over the decades, guarded their patrimony against the kind of settling-up that had taken place in other parts of the west, most notably in Colorado and Wyoming, with the kind of ferocity that prevailed at that time in all the more or less lawless land west of the Missouri River.

And, since all life is to some extent a trade-off, although the early Yaqui settlers had no great admiration for Mexicans, which to them meant anyone who spoke Spanish, the result of an inaccurate lumping of *mestizos, criollos*, and *gachupíns*, they had to, over the years, accept the more numerous Spanish-speaking earlier settlers, and over the decades to intermarry with them, until the earlier contempt became rather a general tolerance. If not quite a general social acceptance, at least an understanding and to some extent an admiration of people of a different race, culture and language, than the Yaqui varieties, whose centuries of adaptation had enabled them to develop the only kind of existence which was compatible with the territory.

The Yaquis became bilingual. As Alan Gardea had once observed, what the *norteamericanos* could not overcome, they adapted to: while in the process appreciating their minority status at the beginning, they had shrewdly made certain that Yaquis would hold the high offices of the territory. The *alcalde* became the mayor, the *juez politico* became His Honour the judge, the *juzgado* became the jail-house and *muy matador* became the gunman, whether he functioned within or without the law.

It was, as Alan Gardea's father had said, a small price to pay for a continued existence in paradise, and with an almost philosophical shrug, he had also said that while conquerors come and go, people who mind their business go on and – and on. After all, Yaquis did not eat natives, their primary objective was identical to those of the earlier owners of this land – to establish large ranches, to flourish and live well; so, perhaps, in time the disparate people would come together. And they had. Alan Gardea's father had been a *gachupín*, his mother had been the sister of a Yaqui cowman-settler named Dougherty. Patrick Maclean Dougherty. Alan had the light hazel eyes, the quick and abiding sensitivity of his father's people, the powerful build and height of his mother's forefathers and the kind of humour which was a meld of both heritages.

In some ways he was like neither; he was not married into his thirtieth year, unheard of among *gachupín* males, viewed askance by his mother's side, and while he was a good stockman, he went to town Saturday nights with the hired men, and he roped with them at the gathering grounds. He also, unacceptably to both heritages, liked those whom he liked regardless of whether they were *mestizos* or more sociably acceptable *criollos* or *gachupínes*. It was this particular trait that made him liked among the *vaqueros*, the *peons*, even the most red-necked of the Yaquis.

He was an easy man to be around, always natural, always predictable, a man of easy temperament – or so it always seemed – imbued with a not-quite-serious, humorous outlook on life that made him welcome in *haciendas* or *jacals*.

Before his father had died, he had told Alan's Irish

mother that their son was the despair of his old age. The father was a dyed-in-the-wool *gachupín*, which was to say he believed as much in a large family whose reunions on special days were the delight of other *gachupín* elders, as he believed in the Holy Church.

Alan's mother, also a believer in grandchildren, had manipulated a number of eligible young girls, and, later, young women – of which there were never many available – to no avail. Her handsome, thoroughly capable and popular son had never allowed female companionship to interfere with his stockman's prerogatives.

Of this at least his father approved; there was no more knowledgeable cowman in all Northern New Mexico, and no more accomplished horseman, but his father had departed this life with that single disappointment, and Alan's mother finally abandoned any pretence of managing to see that her fatherless son met eligible females.

The Gardea holdings ran for miles, even up over into southern Colorado, and southward down into the desert country with its three-months period of good grazing before the interminable heat arrived to shrivel everything that needed water.

Alan had not quite replaced the old *vaqueros*, but each new man he hired was usually a Yaqui. The ranch required six full-time riders, but at least in New Mexico Territory the more northerly custom of having a male cook and a big cookhouse where all the hired people ate, usually together, was replaced by Alan Gardea with the oldtime custom of *mestizo* women cooks and instead of one large bunkhouse, the more fraternal custom of each hired man having his own *jacal*. These differences were easily accepted by the *norteamericano* cowboys. In fact most of them liked the idea of not having to be crowded into one bunkhouse, surviving on the cooking of what were usually old broken-down rangemen like themselves who were passed off as cooks and could not as a rule boil water without burning it.

Alan's *mayordomo*, or rangeboss, was a greying man named John Bristow, who had worked for his father and knew the Gardea range as well as anyone and better than most.

Bristow was a shrewd-eyed, taciturn individual of indeterminate age whose faded blue eyes missed very little and whose ability to handle men had endeared him to Alan's father.

Bristow, it was whispered, had been trying to reach Mexico ahead of a posse of manhunters when he had been taken in by Alan's father and sheltered, and had over the years repaid the elder Gardea with unswerving loyalty.

He had never married, lived in the *jacal* nearest the communal kitchen and dining-hall, and had eventually become bilingual, although he'd never even heard anyone speak Spanish until that summer years earlier when he'd appeared in the Gardea yard, shrunken from hunger, riding a horse which had been ridden almost to the point of foundering.

Now, years later, he could sling the border-Mex lingo with the best of them, his health had recovered, he had put on weight, and the horse that had saved him while the posse-riders had been on his back-trail had not been ridden in ten years; it loafed away the summers in shade and tall grass, and grew plenty of long hair to come through even the worst northern New Mexico winter, unaware that this was John Bristow's way of demonstrating loyalty to creatures – two-legged or four-legged – toward whom he felt a deep and abiding sense of obligation.

It was John Bristow who, while range-riding, saw the head-hung horse and what appeared to be a hasty dry camp south of a place called Escalante Canyon, and who had not approached the camp, although there was no rider in sight, but who had loped up-country several miles to Indian Hill, a knobby hillock with a view of the countryside for miles, and had squatted up there watching, waiting, for movement; and when he saw it finally, miles distant, raising tan dust, had high-tailed it back to the dry camp and this time came on to the owner of that exhausted horse from an *arroyo* and had spoken in English before the man hunkering there had any idea anyone was within miles of him.

Bristow had said, 'Partner, just set easy,' and because he was uncertain whether he was addressing a Mexican or a Yaqui, had said in Spanish; 'Be tranquil, friend and listen.'

The squatting man stiffened, otherwise he did not move. He was bronzed from a lifetime of exposure, lean and wiry with a Colt on his hip which had beautifully carved walnut grips. He kept his back to the man in the *arroyo*.

When Bristow knew the rider was not going to spring up and go for his gun he spoke again. 'There are six riders on your back-trail about two miles north. Now listen to me: saddle and bridle your horse. Don't get on him, lead him toward the sound of my voice. There's a deep *arroyo* over here. Lead him down into it and follow me.'

The squatting man did not move.

Bristow said, 'Unless you want them to overtake you.'

The squatting man arose, brought his animal in,

rigged it out and led it westerly toward the *arroyo* with John Bristow watching everything he did. The man had dark hair and eyes but he was a *norteamericano*. It took John back many years watching the man and the exhausted, ridden-down horse.

Not until the stranger and his animal were in the *arroyo* did they face each other. John said nothing, simply turned and led his horse southward in the deep *arroyo*. The stranger said nothing either, not for several hundred yards where there was a wide washed-out place, and the *arroyo* turned west.

They continued in this new direction for another few hundred yards before John handed the stranger his reins, climbed a crumbly bank and flattened where he could look back.

The riders had reached the dry camp and were milling around talking and gesturing. Bristow slid back down, retrieved his reins and said, 'Partner, this is goin' to be close and your horse don't have much left in him. Mount up and follow me.'

Bristow rode with a cold twinkle in his eyes; this was the identical *arroyo* old Gardea had used many years earlier to lead John Bristow to safety.

For the first time the stranger spoke. 'I'm obliged, mister, but what's your interest?'

All the Gardea rangeboss said was: 'Later,' and led the stranger over the same route the elder Gardea had used to save John Bristow's hide long ago.

Four generations of Gardeas had operated the ranch; inevitably they had discovered the ancient Indian cave with its sooty interior and red-ochre pictographs which was behind a jumble of huge grey boulders, not only very well hidden, but somewhat higher than the floor of the *arroyo*.

What made it particularly attractive to people who

preferred not to be surprised, was that where the bottom of the *arroyo* ran east and west it had over the millennia been scoured by flash-floods down to bedrock so hard and pale it did not even show shod-horse tracks unless someone got down on their knees and traced out each faint little scratch.

It was around through the boulders that John Bristow led the stranger to the entrance of the ancient cave, where they dismounted and led their animals into the dark, cool interior.

Their worry was that the animals might nicker when the six horsemen rode past. In order to ensure this did not happen each man stood at his horse's head ready to clamp down hard.

The stranger said, 'Mister, don't think I'm not grateful, because I am. They'd have caught me sure as hell within the next few hours. My horse was done for. But – who are you, where did you come from an' why was you willin' to take a chance and help me?'

John considered the younger, taller dark-eyed man with a sardonic smile. 'We'll talk when your friends has rode past.'

It was a long wait. The riders were clearly not novices at manhunting. Two of them rode on the land above the *arroyo* on each side and two rode down into the *arroyo*. John saw the two on the south side and heard the opposite pair as they passed through underbrush above the *arroyo*. He could not see the men down in the *arroyo* without going outside, which he did not do.

He offered the stranger a plug of chewing tobacco, which was declined with a head-shake, bit off a cud for himself and smiled a little as he heard men talking.

They lost the tracks where the white granite began.

Overhead, someone called to the men down below. 'Ain't no sign of the son of a bitch up ahead, Alf.'

The reply coming from down in the *arroyo* rang with angry exasperation. 'Well now, goddamit, he didn't sprout wings an' fly. You boys lope ahead. He's got to be up there somewhere.'

John Bristow's smile deepened, he spat aside and winked at the tense stranger. This was almost an exact replay of what had happened years ago, and John did as the elder Gardea had done back then; he waited a half-hour to be sure the manhunters were a considerable distance off, then led his companion back down into the *arroyo*, retracing their own tracks to a slope leading up to the higher, open country, and headed straight for the home-place.

It was a long ride and both mounted men sat half-twisted watching for pursuit: Bristow did not believe there would be any, and he was correct. But – seasoned manhunters would probably back-track, find where two horsemen had come up out of the *arroyo* and headed southeast. And sure as the Good Lord had made green apples, they would eventually ride into the large compound of the Gardea ranch.

That too had happened before. As John Bristow rode it was like a re-enactment. He smiled, spat amber a few times and when they had the yard in sight he loosened in the saddle and said, 'Well now, *amigo*, up ahead they'll want to know your name.'

The stranger lifted his hat, scratched, re-set his hat and smiled at John for the first time. 'That's quite a set of buildings,' he said admiringly, then answered the question. 'I sure as hell owe you, mister. My name is Charley Schilling.'

Bristow nodded. He'd expected the name to be John Smith or Tom Jones. Charley Schilling was not the kind of name a fugitive would pick out of the blue. It was a good start. As John eyed the activity in the big yard he said, 'Charley, this is the Gardea ranch. They been here since before we got New Mexico from the Mexicans. It's run different from most places rangemen been. They're good to work for ... You speak any Spanish?'

'No. I have trouble with English. They're Messicans?'

'You ever been down here before?'

'No. Never been south of Wyoming before.'

'Well, let's commence your education right now. The Gardeas aren't Mexicans. They're what're known as *gachupins*. It simply means "wearers of spurs", which is what the native Mexicans called Spaniards. These folk are Spanish, not Mex. I know, they pretty much look alike, but don't ever make the mistake of tellin' one you thought he was a Mexican.'

John Bristow jettisoned his cud, tipped back his hat and made a final sweep of their back-trail before settling forward on the outskirts of the tree-shaded big ranch yard.

'Charley, I been down here a long time. The reason I helped you was because the older Gardea saved my hide exactly as I saved yours today; used the same cave, an' later, when riders come nosin' around, he hid me until they left.'

Charley Schilling had a hard sound to his words when he said, 'You're rangeboss here?' and when John Bristow nodded the stranger also said, 'Boss, those fellers aren't goin' to just ride away. They been on my butt since Colorado.'

2 Charley's Story

Alan Gardea listened carefully to everything John Bristow had to say, and fixed his rangeboss with a quizzical little smile. 'Old times, John?'

Bristow nodded, and waited.

'Where is he?'

Bristow pointed toward the low-roofed, big horse barn.

They walked over there together, entered the shadows where sunlight hadn't reached in a hundred years and John said, 'Charley?'

The raw-boned, lean man appeared out of a horse stall. He and Alan regarded each other. Alan held out his hand. 'I'm Alan Gardea.'

The stranger pumped the hand once and released it. 'Charley Schilling, Mister Gardea.'

Alan turned to his rangeboss. 'Look after his animal, John. We'll be over at the house.'

As they crossed the yard *mestizo* women eyed them askance, and the few men still in the yard at this time of day did the same, but until they had passed through a high adobe wall into a patio with red tile and a huge old shade tree neither man spoke. Alan gestured toward a long bench and sat down upon the circular stone wall around the big old shade tree. He studied the stranger for a moment before saying, 'Where did John find you?'

'North of here near a deep *arroyo*.'

'And took you to the old Indian cave?'

'Yes.'

Alan eased back until his shoulders were against the tree trunk. 'How many are looking for you?'

'Six.'

'Lawmen, are they?'

'Well, one is, the others are hired posse-riders. They been pretty close the last few days, my horse was giving out.'

'How long, Charley?'

Schilling shrugged. 'I don't keep track of time very good. About five, six weeks. I didn't know it until I was 'way south into Colorado.'

Alan looked toward the gateless opening in the patio wall. 'Charley, we have law too. If those riders go to our nearest town, which is about four miles from here, they'll look up the sheriff ... Tell me straight out, Charley: is there a reward out for you?'

'Well, there may be by now, I don't know.'

'For what?'

Charley Schilling also looked in the direction of the gateless opening, beyond which was the sun-drenched big yard with its shaggy old trees and little houses among other out-buildings. 'I killed a man up in Wyoming.'

'Fair fight?'

'Well ... not exactly. He wasn't armed.'

'Did you know he wasn't armed?'

'It was dark, Mister Gardea,' the stranger said with a drag in his voice.

'Did you know him?'

'Yes ... he didn't usually wear a gun.'

'You knew that when you killed him?'

'Yes sir, I knew it.'

John Bristow appeared in the gateless opening, ignored Schilling and addressed Alan Gardea.

'They're coming. Six of them.'

Alan stood up. 'Put him in the pit, John, then come to the barn.'

Bristow nodded. 'Want the men to be there?'

'No. Just you'n me.'

The rangeboss jerked his head and Charley Schilling nodded to Alan Gardea before following the rangeboss back across the yard.

Others in the yard had seen the dust raised by horsemen, and all the women and several of the men got inside buildings.

What Alan Gardea had called 'the pit' was a cellar-type dugout about twelve feet square which, during earlier times, had been the refuge of the Gardeas and their hired people during Indian raids. There was an old ladder made of poles with rungs held in place by rawhide. Bristow held the trapdoor open and gestured for Charley Schilling to use the ladder. It bent under his weight and when he was down there with the only light coming from above, John Bristow said, 'Don't make a sound. When I come back I'll stamp four times on the opening.'

The moment he closed the concealed trapdoor Charley Schilling couldn't see his hand in front of his face. He listened for sounds, but the Second Coming could have occurred in the yard, complete with golden trumpets, and he couldn't have heard any of it.

John Bristow went over to the long tie-rack in front of the barn and leaned there with Alan Gardea watching the oncoming riders, who were approaching at a dead walk as they studied the yard, the buildings, the few individuals who were visible.

Alan said, 'The shaggy-headed man in front has a badge.'

John nodded. 'Big enough to eat hay. It'd take a lot of changing horses to keep him on a manhunt.'

Alan nodded. He was studying the other five riders. They were travel-stained, grim-faced and heavily armed. 'Somebody,' Gardea told his range-boss, 'wants Charley Schilling pretty bad.'

The only sound as the strangers crossed the yard was made by the shod hooves of their horses and the whisper of un-oiled saddle leather.

The large man in the lead with a badge on his shirtfront was greying, bearded and coarse-featured. As with the others he was armed with a belt-gun and an up-ended carbine on the right side.

When he stopped and rested both hands atop the saddlehorn as he studied Bristow and Gardea, he said, 'I'm Deputy Sheriff Comstock. These gents with me are possemen. We been on the trail of a murderer named Schilling for a long time ... His tracks seem to lead to this yard.'

Alan Gardea leaned on the tie-rack and did not move nor raise his voice when he replied. 'How do you tell one set of tracks from another, Deputy? My riders have been going in and out of the yards for days.'

The big bearded man's attitude changed slightly when he answered. 'Well now, mister, the tracks we followed come from a canyon where Schilling an' someone else hid until we went past, then come down this way.' Comstock shifted slightly in his saddle. 'Mister Whateveryourname is, Schilling is a murderer. He killed a man in cold blood in Wyoming. We're not goin' back without him.'

Alan Gardea nodded slightly. 'It's been a long ride for you, Deputy.'

'Yes it has, an' we're going to keep right on.'

'It must be a large reward, Deputy,' Alan said quietly, and Comstock's eyes narrowed slightly. 'Maybe by now there is, I don't know. We took up the trail the day after the killing.'

Alan gave another of those slight nods. 'In defence of the law – or because you were hired to find Schilling?'

Comstock, a bull of a man unaccustomed to being questioned, leaned on his saddlehorn. 'What's your name, mister?'

'Alan Gardea.'

'You own this ranch, do you?'

'Yes.'

Comstock leaned back off the saddlehorn. 'I heard this here is Mex-country, Mister Gardea. I also heard the law ain't much down here.'

John Bristow spoke for the first time. 'Let me give you some advice,' he told the large man. 'Learn the customs of this country and be real careful with your mouth. The law down here is as good as it is in Wyoming. Unless you want to make trouble, then you might find that it's a little different.'

Comstock and his five hard-faced possemen regarded Bristow coldly. One of the riders said, 'I've heard Messican law is good at back-shooting.'

Bristow straightened up off the rack but Alan replied to the posseman. 'You gents are makin' a real good start at finding out how things work down here.'

Comstock looked past, into the shadowy interior of the barn. He saw several moving shadows back down there and used discretion when next he spoke. 'Tell me flat out, Mister Gardea: Schilling is a tall feller, dark in the face an' ridin' a bad-off horse. He's a murderer an' we want him ... Have you seen anyone answerin' his description?'

Alan's reply was forthright. 'If we see anyone like that we'll let you know. The nearest town is south-east of here about four miles. You can put up over there. In English the name of the town is Nowhere. The sheriff is a man named Burt Evans.'

For a moment the possemen sat gazing at the pair of men behind the tie-rack, then Comstock turned without a nod or another word and led off out of the yard.

Bristow watched them riding southeast and spat into the dust. 'You know them kind, Alan?'

Gardea slapped his rangeboss on the shoulder as he replied. 'Maybe not as well as you do, John, but yes, I know their kind.'

As Bristow turned to enter the barn he said, 'They're trouble,' and Alan Gardea shrugged.

The following morning a horseman appeared in the yard shortly after the riders had left and the women were cleaning up after an earlier meal. He rode directly to the house, swung off, loped his reins through a stud-ring embedded in the thick adobe wall, crossed the patio and rattled the massive, bolt-studded oaken front door. When it opened a startled *mestizo* woman said, 'Wait, *Señor*,' and disappeared into the house. Moments later Alan Gardea appeared with a smile. He took the visitor to the identical place where he and Charley Schilling had sat the day before and said, 'You had visitors last night. I told them you'd be in town and told them your name.'

Sheriff Burt Evans nodded. 'Comstock's a tough man, Alan. He thinks you got this Schilling feller on the ranch.'

'Does he have a warrant for him, Burt?'

'Well ... not one that's worth a damn in New

Mexico,' the sheriff replied and eased back a little. 'If he's here long enough he can send up to Wyoming for the governor up there to contact our governor over in Santa Fé ... You got Schilling, Alan?'

'Burt, I have to know more. If he doesn't come up with the right answers today, I'll bring him to town.'

'Accordin' to that big deputy he's a murderer, Alan. You're takin' chances out here.'

'We've been taking chances out here since before my grandfather's day ... You had breakfast?'

'Yeah. Before I left town.'

'Did they put up at the hotel?'

'Yes. What worries me is that they might stay a while, and any way a man looks at it, Alan, they are trouble.' As the sheriff arose he said, 'You can point Schilling towards the border, start him out at night an' maybe give him some grub.'

As they moved from the patio to the lawman's patient-standing horse, Alan Gardea said, 'I could do that. But if he's really a murderer I'll bring him to town.'

As Sheriff Evans was leaving the yard Alan Gardea's mother came to the patio and was waiting when Alan returned. She was a handsome woman with a flawless complexion, eyes as blue as cornflowers. She had a trace of grey over the temples but otherwise looked ten years younger than her fifty years.

Dorotea Gardea – christened Dorothy Dougherty – was a direct woman. When her son appeared in the gateless patio entrance she said, 'What is it, Alan?' and her son smiled, stepped into the shade and told her. She listened, did not look away from her son and finally said, 'Your father did the same thing once.'

'Yes, with John Bristow.'

'But they aren't all like John, Alan ... a murderer?'

'*Quién es*?'

'Where do you have him?'

'In the pit yesterday when those northern lawmen rode in. Today in the *jacal* where Tiburcio used to live.'

'Alan ...!'

'Mother, I talked to him, right here on the patio, yesterday. One thing I feel sure of is that he is not a liar.'

'How do you know?'

Alan smiled at his mother. 'I guess the same way my father knew the same thing with John.'

'And ...?'

'I'm going to talk to him again today. If my hunch is bad I'll take him to town and hand him over to Burt. If it's not ...'

'You can't hire him, Alan. Not with lawmen looking for him. It will cause trouble. We've had all we can do with the ranch ... Alan?'

He took her hand and walked to the bolt-studded oaken door and released her hand. 'I'll talk to him now, and come back here afterward.'

Dorotea Gardea watched her son stride across the patio out into the yard. An older, very dark *mestizo* woman appeared soundlessly and spoke in Spanish. 'Men! They are God's curse to women.'

The *jacal* where John Bristow had installed Charley Schilling was old, full of cobwebs, with a *caliche* floor as hard as rock, one small window without glass and a corner combination fireplace and cooking area.

Charley Schilling was using an old broom to wipe away spider webs when Alan entered, watched for a moment then said, 'If you had a fire we could have coffee.' He pointed to a dented old coffee pot and sat on a bench beside the door.

Schilling's reply was basic. 'If I had some coffee … I saw the gent on the sorrel horse with the badge. Is he the local law?'

'Yes. Burt Evans. He met the Wyoming riders last night. Tell me a little more, Charley. Yesterday you didn't seem sorry for the murder. Can I ask why?'

Schilling pulled around an old hand-made chair with a sagging rawhide seat and faced Alan Gardea as he spoke. 'Yesterday I didn't think you'd be interested in the reason, and we didn't have a whole lot of time to talk.'

'We have time now,' Alan replied.

Charley leaned with both hands clasped and said, 'It goes back about nine years. My folks came to Wyoming from Illinois to take up some railroad land. The winters were hard but the three of us worked hard; my paw, my maw an' me. We had two good crop-years, bought some livestock and was really settling in …'

'And?'

'You sure you want to hear all this, Mister Gardea?'

'Yes I'm sure.'

'My folks bought an adjoining homestead from a man named Bradley. It had a runnin' spring that flowed year round. What Mister Bradley never told my paw was that a cowman who claimed the adjoining land had been starvin' Bradley for two years to get the land, and the spring. Mostly the spring. He was mad as hell when Bradley told him he'd sold out to us.

'Hiram Foster was a mean-spirited son of a bitch. He didn't like folks, but mostly homesteaders. He called Paw out one night an' when Paw came back he was white in the face. Foster had told Paw he'd give what we gave Bradley for the land. Paw refused and Foster told him before another year passed Paw'd wish to hell he'd sold.

'That winter our hay barn full of a summer's feed burnt to the ground in the night. After Christmas four of our work-horses was found shot dead. Before spring came my mother broke down. I took her to town for the midwife to look after. There wasn't a doctor anywhere close.

'She died just as the wildflowers was blooming. She used to like to walk out a mile or so among them … When it was time to put in a grain crop I didn't have harness horses to break the ground with. I tried to trade for some in town an' the horsetrader refused to sell or trade any work-horses to me. I took him out in the alley and lit into him. He squawked like a stuck pig and told me Hiram Foster had told him not to sell me horses no matter what.

'Paw never recovered after Maw died. I did the best I could do that year an' he gave up and died that autumn.'

'Did Foster get the land?'

'Yes; at a forced sale. He rode into the yard one day to show me the deed and told me I had two days to leave. He laughed when I said I couldn't do it all in two days. He had two men with him. He said two days or I'd get what my folks got.'

'You left?'

'Yes. Sold off what I had and went to ridin' for some cow outfits. The more I thought back the more I wanted to settle with that son of a bitch.

'I went back, waited until he was leavin' the saloon one night, caught him at the edge of town, told him to get down off his horse because I was goin' to beat half the life out of him. He started screaming curses at me and spurred his horse …'

'And you shot him in the back?'

Charley Schilling nodded without looking up. 'It

was murder for a fact, Mister Gardea. The law don't care about reasons, only that I shot Foster in the back … I lit out headin' for Mexico. Foster's son hired that deputy and those riders to track me down an' either kill me or fetch me back where he'd make sure I got hanged.'

Alan sat a moment regarding the tall, raw-boned man, then shot up to his feet. 'Charley, I'll stake you to a good horse, some money and some grub and point you toward Mexico. Stay down there for a year or two, then come back if you want to.'

Charley Schilling also arose. 'I'll pay for the horse and grub,' he said. 'An' I'd like to thank your rangeboss before I go.'

Alan nodded about that. 'We'll talk again after nightfall.'

'Mister Gardea, I'm grateful for all you've done.'

Alan smiled and said, '*Por nada,*' as he left the *jacal* to cross in the direction of the main house where his mother was waiting.

3 Augustino Madrigal

It showed clearly in Dorotea Gardea's face that she was enormously relieved after Alan had told her his decision about Charley Schilling.

She patted his hand and went to the kitchen where her cook was preparing a meal. They talked in Spanish for a while.

Alan waited until John Bristow returned with the riders then explained that they would give Charley

Schilling a strong horse, some money and food and aim him toward Mexico. Bristow's quizzical expression prompted Gardea to say, 'I believe him, John. A year from now if he returns we'll hire him. But six of them with the law on their side could make things bad for us right at a time when we'll be working cattle.'

Bristow shrugged, went to Schilling's *jacal* and they talked for a half-hour, until dusk was settling, then Bristow went to the big circular pole horse-corral out behind the barn, selected a powerfully built, pig-eyed, dun gelding and led it into the barn.

There was only a sliver of a moon when Alan and John rode out of the yard heading south with Charley Schilling between them. Conversation was desultory for a mile, then Charley Schilling told Alan Gardea he would pay him for the horse, and that he didn't need any money, and was grateful for the grub and the inconvenience he had put them all to.

Alan smiled. 'The horse is a gift. We have two hundred horses. As for the rest of it, *gracias por nada*. Do you understand?'

'No.'

'Well, in English it sort of means thank me for nothing. In other words, you're welcome and good luck.'

They halted near a tiny mud *jacal* with a powerful scent of goats where a feeble light showed from a glassless window, told Charley Schilling to hold to his present course and with the good horse under him he should reach the border in a couple of days. They shook hands all around and Charley rode south. Alan and his rangeboss sat until they could no longer hear a moving animal, then turned back.

It was close to midnight when they reached the yard and cared for their mounts. At the tie-rack out front John said, 'Good night,' in Spanish. He and his employer exchanged a long look and parted.

The following day Alan rode with his riders to begin a big sweep to bring cattle to the marking ground, which was roughly a mile northwest of the yard near Escalante Canyon. It was one of those chores that required at least a week of hard riding. The purpose of the gather was to mark late calves, ones dropped since the early spring gather.

Branding and ear-marking was no guarantee that cattle would not be rustled. Every time there was an insurrection down in Old Mexico *guerrilleros*, the destitute rebels, raided north of the line for cattle to feed their armies. They did not ordinarily raid as far north as the Gardea holdings, but that usually depended on whether they found cattle closer to the border.

Over the generations the Gardeas had lost cattle to *pronunciados* from Old Mexico, rampaging Indians of several different tribes, fierce and deadly *norteamericano* rustlers, and even to outlaws running for the border who took a few head to make entrance into Old Mexico easier.

Three days into the round-up John Bristow sat with Alan Gardea watching the hundreds of beeves fanning out in the vicinity of the marking ground, and said, 'This here is the third year our tally come up with the right number. Rustlin' is maybe goin' out of style.'

Alan smiled. Both of them knew better. When the riders came along everyone headed for the yard. It was close enough to the end of the day to call it quits until sun-up.

It was late with only a few candles showing among the *jacals* when a raggedy-pantsed *peon* riding a large *burro* entered the yard and roused several dogs less with their sounds than with their smell.

Lights sputtered here and there. Over at the main-house Maria the hefty *mestizo* cook and protector of her mistress awakened, cursed, padded toward the back of the house to awaken her mistress.

Dorotea and Maria listened to the tumult in the yard and heard harsh voices raised in Spanish toward someone. Dorotea sent Maria to awaken Alan. The hefty *mestiza*, who had been the first to see Alan after the midwife had delivered him, shook him roughly and said, 'Someone is in the yard … If it is another like the last one, add no more grey hair to your mother, chase him away.'

Alan got out of bed, dressed without haste and was not completely awake and alert until he was buckling his shellbelt into place on the way to the patio.

John Bristow was entering the gateless opening into the patio when Alan stepped out into the pre-dawn chill. When the rangeboss saw Alan he turned, grabbed someone by the shoulder and propelled him through the gateway.

Alan knew the old, very dark and weathered old man with the strong smell of goats. He greeted him curtly and said, 'What is it, *viejo*?'

The old *peon* crushed an ancient hat to his chest as he replied. '*Patrón*, I didn't know what to do. Your yard was closer than town so I came here.'

Alan nodded for the old man to be seated and asked John to get a glass of wine from the house. As Bristow disappeared beyond the massive oaken door the old man made a tentative smile and spoke in slow Spanish. 'It was late, *Patrón*. I thought I heard coyotes and was awake listening, because they kill my animals. But it was riders. I could hear steel horseshoes over stones.'

John returned, handed the glass of dark wine to the old man and stood hip-shot, thumbs hooked in his shellbelt until the old man had swallowed several times before resuming his tale. 'I blew out my candle, *Señores*, and stood by the window with my old gun. There were three of them out a distance. They talked then one of them rode south and the other two sat until he was gone then turned back northward.'

John and Alan exchanged a look. They had seen the candle and had smelled the goats even though they had not been close to the *jacal*.

The old man crossed himself as he put the wine aside. 'Maybe an hour later, maybe more, I heard gunshots. For no reason, *Señores*; all of a sudden gunshots in the middle of the night. South of my house, but loud.'

John was scowling. 'You went out there?'

The old man looked incredulous. 'No, *jefe*. I am an old man who lives alone and minds his goats. There was more than one shooter down there ... No, not until dawn ...' The old man drained the glass before continuing. '*Señores*, there was two dead men ... I thought because both were lying in blood. But one was not quite dead. He was too heavy so I didn't try to get him on to my *burro*. I made a blanket with ropes and took him to my house. The other one was dead, shot through the middle of his chest. Very dead.'

John Bristow went to the stone circle around the old shade tree and sat down. In Spanish he said, 'This one who was not dead – he looked like what?'

The old man stood up and raised a hand above his head. 'Tall, *jefe*,' he lowered the hand. 'He was riding a big strong dun horse.' The old man sat back down. 'The horse is still down there. Very dead.'

Bristow and Alan Gardea stared at the old man.

When the rangeboss stood up he addressed his employer in English. 'The sons of bitches were watching, Alan.'

Gardea did not speak for a long while, not until he had sat on the stone wall around the old trees from which his rangeboss had just arisen. 'It'll be daylight in a few hours,' he mused aloud, and looked at his rangeboss. 'If you took a wagon down there and brought him back – if he's still alive – they'll be watching, John, sure as hell.'

Bristow's face was dark with anger. 'Good. I'll take the riders with me. If they're still down there we'll make them wish to Chris' they'd never come down here.'

Alan stood up shaking his head. 'No, not that way. It'll start a war.'

'How then?'

Alan was quiet for a moment or two, then he said, 'I'll go back with the old man. Never mind the marking ground today, keep the riders in the yard until I return. If he's dead I'll come back before afternoon.'

'And if he ain't dead?'

Alan looked out into the dark yard past the gateless opening in the patio wall. 'Be very careful, John. Don't approach the *jacal*, sift around down there. If they're not there, then come to the *jacal* and we'll bring him back here.'

John sounded disgusted when he said, 'Alan, if they lost a man down there, they'll be around.'

'You flush them out,' Gardea replied. 'John, any way you look at it, there's going to be trouble. If you don't find them, come to the house and we'll bring Schilling back here – if he's alive. If he's dead it won't matter, they can have the corpse. We'll have done all we could do for him.' The old man, who had only a very slight command of English, looked from Alan to John Bristow wearing a worried look. As he too arose he said, '*Señores*, this came to me without my expecting it. Please – I live apart with my old *burro*, my goat, some chickens ...'

Alan patted the old man on the shoulder. 'We'll take the wounded one away. The dead one, I think his friends will come for. Stay away from down there for a few days. If they bother you, let me know.'

The old *peon* was not quite relieved but he said no more as John Bristow left the patio and Alan Gardea walked with the old man to his big *burro*, told him to wait, and continued on over to the barn to saddle and bridle a horse.

It was cold. The old man had a threadbare *serape* which he wound about his upper body and Alan Gardea freed the jacket aft of his cantle and shrugged into it as he and the old man rode southward.

They said very little. Alan knew of the old man, had known of him since his youth, but did not know his name, which the old man told him was Augustino Madrigal. As he said this he smiled for the first time. He did not know where the name had originated. As he told Alan, Madrigal had something to do with music, he knew that, but he knew little about music and could play no musical instrument.

Daylight was coming, they knew that because it always was coldest just before sunrise. When they could see the *jacal* some goats were bleating, which the old man said was their custom when they thought it was time to be taken forth to browse.

To Alan the bleating suggested that no one was close by. He left the old man at his house and rode southward for almost a mile before he found the dead dun horse and the man with the bullet hole in its fatal place. He rolled the man on to his back, recognized him as one of the Wyoming posse-riders, went to look at the horse, the innocent victim of those he had served in life without ever completely trusting them, and rode back to the *jacal* with the dead posseman's carbine and sixgun, and the flat leather wallet from the man's trouser pocket.

The old man was outside when Alan tied up and entered the *jacal*. There was a candle burning on an old table. A scarred old long-barrelled rifle was lying on it.

The *jacal* was furnished like most were; it had a bed built against one wall, a corner fireplace and cooking area, shelves with bottles and tins on them, a bucket of water near the door, and one picture of the Crucified Christ on the wall above some painstakingly harvested grass seeds and dried grass, feed for the old man's livestock when winter grazing was poor.

Charley Schilling was a gory mess atop an ancient tan army blanket in the middle of the floor. He had been shot once across the top of his shoulder, which bled a lot but did not seem to Alan Gardea to amount to much of a threat to his life. The second wound was more serious. It had not bled as much but there was a swelling, bluish puckered place on the right side where a bullet had entered, and in back where it had exited the hole was ragged.

Alan looked around for some kind of liquor and found a bottle of *pulque* on a shelf. As he was pouring a little into a cracked old crockery cup the old man returned. Alan asked if he'd seen anything and the old man shook his head as he watched Alan kneel to tip *pulque* past the grey lips of the injured man.

The old man crossed himself. In his long life he

had seen wounded men. When they were as inert and as bloody as this one, they died.

Charley Schilling swallowed twice. Alan sat back waiting, then tipped more *pulque* past the slack lips and arose as the old man busied himself building a small, warming fire of dry mesquite.

Schilling coughed weakly and Alan sank to one knee. The old man handed him the candle to be held close in case there was a sign of life. There was none, Charley remained unconscious, but his colouring improved a little. Alan put the candle aside, stood up and told the old man to keep watch over the injured man, while he scouted around outside.

The old man obeyed, but with a forehead creased with anxiety.

Dawn was coming. Alan ignored the curious stares of the goats, saw the old man's *burro* lipping up whatever he could find that was edible, heard chickens in a tightly-made little round faggot fence, and went out into the scattered underbrush a fair distance. He did not expect to be confronted. If that happened this morning it would be later. He looked for shod-horse sign and found it only when he angled south-westerly out a distance from the *jacal*.

Evidently the spy had known when Schilling and his companions left the ranch yard riding south. Equally probable, it had taken time for the watcher, or watchers, to find deputy Comstock and the other possemen, and bring them down here.

Alan stood a while taking the pulse of the pre-dawn paleness before returning to the *jacal*. Of one thing he was certain: Comstock and his riders would return. They had lost a man and that would concern them. If they were still around when John Bristow and the Gardea riders came along, there would be a fight. John Bristow lived in a world of black and white. You did or you didn't. If you did, it was in defence of something you believed in. Bristow may have told Alan's father of his past but neither his father nor John Bristow had ever mentioned it to Alan.

Over the years, though, Alan had come to understand how John Bristow regarded the world, and as he was approaching the *jacal* in the growing pink of a new day, he hoped that Comstock and his riders would not be out here when Bristow came scouting for them.

Augustino Madrigal was holding a cup of goat-meat broth in his hand as Alan entered the *jacal*. The man he had been about to feed this to, swung his eyes, recognized Gardea and closed his eyes.

Alan held him up as the old man fed him hot broth. It seemed to have a better effect than the *pulque* had. Charley Schilling made a feeble smile and whispered, 'I heard them before they saw me.'

'Six of them?'

'Five. Comstock was not down here with them … I was trying to reach a thicket of chaparral when they started firing. The horse went down and I got behind him. They spread out and I shot one off his horse. The others fired back, then left. They thought I was dead. Or they didn't have no stomach for going up against a man who was forted up.'

For a long time Schilling lay back breathing shallowly. Eventually he looked up at Gardea and said, 'How did they know?'

'Spying on the yard, most likely. Otherwise they couldn't have known. Only John, you and I knew.'

'But it was dark.'

Alan nodded about that as he said, 'Three shod

horses make sounds. Don't bother about that right now. The rangeboss will be along after a while, with the riders. We'll take you back to the ranch.'

Schilling closed his eyes again and the old man was going back over to feed more burls into his fire when Schilling spoke without looking up. 'Go back, Mister Gardea. It'll be over with directly. You done more than enough, but go back.'

Alan considered the improved colour of the wounded man. 'I'm betting you'll make it.'

'I don't feel like I will. Go back and ...'

'Depends on how much blood you lost, Charley. My guess is that although you look like a butchered hog, you didn't lose all that much. Otherwise your colour wouldn't look as good as it does. Sleep now. We'll look after you and wait for John and the riders.'

The old man wanted to take his goats to graze but was afraid to. Alan helped him carry several sacks of dry fodder to the corral and that, at least, stopped the bleating. The old man lingered to draw buckets of water from a dug well and sluice them into an old wooden trough that only leaked at one end.

The sun climbed, heat came, and at least inside the *jacal* with its three-feet thick mud walls, when the old man's fire died, the house remained cool.

Alan watched Charley Schilling pass from consciousness to unconsciousness until, in early afternoon the conscious periods were longer. He and the old man fed Charley more hot broth, which seemed to help him more than anything else.

By mid-afternoon his periods of awareness were much longer. He was as weak as a kitten. The old man heated some water and removed the sticky shirt to bathe Schilling. He was surprisingly gentle, particularly around the areas which were bluish and swollen where the bullet had entered and exited.

Shadows were puddling behind the *jacal* when the wounded man said, 'I think I got one. He went off his horse like a sack of wet grain.'

Alan nodded. 'You did. Remember the broad-faced posseman with the bear-trap mouth and little grey eyes? That's the one. You hit him full on. He was dead before he hit the ground.'

'What did you do with him?'

'Nothing. He's down there near your dead horse. In plain sight if his friends come looking for him.'

Alan stepped to the glassless window, considered the position of the sun, then went to stand in the doorway in shadows studying as much of the area around the *jacal* as he could.

There was not a sound. Not even any cactus wrens. Neither was there any movement.

4 *En Ninguna Parte*

Alan was with the wounded man when a flurry of ragged gunshots erupted. They seemed not to be in any order, as though the gunmen had been either surprised or moving in haste when the firing began.

Alan went to the windows, saw blurry movement to the east and lost it as silence settled. Augustino Madrigal remained away from the door and the window until Alan turned with a shrug. He wasn't sure who had been running but he thought it unlikely that it would be his *vaqueros*, and he was correct.

Half an hour later four horsemen rode up to the

jacal; they dismounted but only one approached the *jacal*. He called ahead. 'Alan?'

Gardea appeared in the doorway as John Bristow shook his head. 'They was out there. They had a dead man tied across a horse when we converged on them. They ran like rabbits. No one got hurt as far as I know. None of us did.'

Alan stepped outside. The sun was no longer climbing. This time of year the days were shorter, which meant before they could return to the home-place dusk would have settled.

Bristow asked if Schilling was dead. Alan shook his head. 'Not yet, but he's been hit hard. Make a travois, John. We'll take him back with us.'

The old man appeared in the doorway. Bristow nodded in his direction. 'He better come with us, Alan. Like it or not, he's involved.'

Alan turned as John jerked his head for the riders to help him find material for a travois. The old man looked frightened. Alan told him in Spanish he should ride north with them to the Gardea ranch, and the old man made a wide gesture with both arms. '*Patrón*; my goats, my chickens ...'

Alan pushed past into the *jacal*, paused to look at the wounded man, then turned and addressed the old man. '*Viejo*, it's your life I'm thinking about. Put more feed into the corral for the goats and scatter something for the chickens. Maybe we can return tomorrow. Get your *burro*. Shortly we will leave.'

It was an hour before they could leave, and the travois that had been cobbled together was serviceable but crude. They carried Charley Schilling to it, did their best to tightly bandage his injuries to minimize more bleeding and, with Augustino Madrigal bringing up the rear, started riding.

The day was dying but it did so slowly. There was coolness in it, which would turn to chill later, but not until they got back to the yard.

John Bristow scattered his riders on both sides to make certain there would be no ambush. There wasn't; evidently being surprised as they came for their dead companion had worked like a physic. There was no sign of riders all the way back to the Gardea compound where Charley Schilling was taken to the main-house while three riders and the rangeboss led the horses away to be cared for.

Maria Escobar met Alan on the patio, stared at the man being carried to the house, rolled her eyes and said in Spanish, 'Why in here? Look at him. For a man to die inside a house is to invite *fantasmas*. Your mother ...'

'Just hold the door wide, Maria. I don't think he will die.'

The dark and burly *mestizo* woman watched them carry Charley Schilling inside with a look of strong disapproval. She followed them as the riders carried Schilling to the rear of the house where there were spare bedrooms, and placed him gently on a bed.

Maria rolled her eyes. The man was bloody, half-dead, dirty. Blood did not wash out of bedding easily if at all. She departed to seek her mistress and tell her what they had done.

Alan lighted two candles, the men who had carried the wounded man to this room departed and when Dorotea Gardea came to the doorway and stopped stone-still gazing toward the bed, the stocky *mestizo* was behind her showing her disapproval but saying nothing as her mistress approached the bed, met the dull gaze of Charley Schilling and said, 'Alan, someone will have to go for the doctor.'

The limp figure on the bed made a small smile at her and whispered a reply. 'They should have left me down there.'

'Down where?' Dorotea asked but Schilling's eyes were closed. Alan told her the entire story. She listened with both hands clasped over her stomach. When he'd finished she turned toward the dark *mestizo* and spoke in Spanish. 'Hot water, Maria. Some clean cloth.'

Maria departed without a sound, but as she set water to boil and rummaged for bandaging material she swore to herself. As with the old goat-herder, she knew the feeling of approaching trouble, and resented very much that her mistress's son was the cause of bringing it into the yard.

Alan watched his mother with mild surprise. She bathed Charley Schilling's upper body, dried it, examined the shoulder wound and bandaged it after sprinkling a disinfectant powder over the gash. She neither looked up nor spoke as she worked, until Maria a dark, stocky shadow, soundlessly came to her side, then all she said was, 'This one is very bad,' in Spanish, and Maria grimly inclined her head.

They had to tip Charley Schilling on to his side to snip away ragged flesh in back, make a compress and wrap his body. Fortunately he was unconscious. As they eased him on to his back again Maria unceremoniously removed his boots and his trousers.

Alan went out to the yard, but there were no lights showing, so he returned to the parlour as Maria entered from the opposite direction. She glared at him as she carried the basin of bloody water to the kitchen.

Alan wondered what John Bristow had done with the old man, Augustino Madrigal, got himself a glass of dark wine and returned to the patio with it.

His mother appeared, drying her hands on a towel. She said, 'He needs the doctor.'

Alan nodded about that. 'I'll go … I didn't know you could handle something like that.'

She came out and sat next to him. 'Before you were born and while you were a baby I had a lot of experience. Your father used to tease me; I delivered babies, cured injuries and sicknesses. He called me his *curandera*.'

Alan offered the glass to his mother; she shook her head, and smiled. 'Maria is furious.'

Alan shrugged. 'What would she have done with a wounded man?'

'The same thing. You exasperate her, Alan.'

He nodded. 'I know. When I was little she'd take after me with a broom. In those days she was fast and not so heavy.'

'You were the apple of her eye, Alan.'

'Was.'

'You still are, but she can't use a broom any more.' Dorotea leaned back. It was late and slightly chilly. 'I don't know; he lost a lot of blood. If he dies what can be done? Bury him in the ranch graveyard? He is a handsome man, Alan.'

Gardea turned slowly and stared at his mother. She was looking skyward. In the soft light she was young again.

Alan stood up. 'I'm tired.'

Dorotea arose and went inside with him. They parted in the parlour, Alan to bed down, his mother to return to the bedroom where two candles burned.

John Bristow was irritable the following morning. It bothered him that after a week of saddlebacking, getting the cattle to the marking ground, unless something was done they would drift farther off and would have to be rounded up all over again.

But he did not mention this when he and Alan met in the yard. All John said was, 'I put the old man up in the shed behind the cookhouse. That *burro* of his was eating his head off when I left him in a corral last night. I don't think he slept last night. When one of the riders pitched a flake to him he was still lipping up twigs from last night.'

Alan laughed. 'Browse never took the place of decent feed. I doubt if he's had anything but brush to pick over most of his life.'

'Alan, somebody should go for the doctor … an' some of the men better go check for drift.'

A burly *mestizo vaquero* came out of the barn, nodded to the *patrón* and the rangeboss and started past when John called to him. 'Juan, see that the goat herder is fed.'

As the stocky *vaquero* turned back in the direction of the cookhouse Alan said, 'I'll go for the doctor. You head for the marking ground with the men.'

Bristow's broad, low forehead wrinkled. 'Not alone, Alan. I'll send the riders out, then ride to town with you.'

Gardea gazed at the worried countenance of his foreman. 'You ride out with them, John. I'll ride to town. There won't be any trouble.'

Bristow's scowl remained. 'We thought that when we took Charley Schilling south in the dark. Alan; Comstock sure as hell's figured things out.'

'It's open country between the ranch and town. Don't worry.'

Bristow did not pursue the topic but he followed Alan to the barn and watched as the younger man rigged out a horse, and shook his head as Alan led the horse out front, swung up and rode south-easterly in the cool morning.

Visibility was perfect; autumn in this part of New Mexico was a lingering time of summer's end and winter's beginning. There were few trees to show russet, yellow and brown leaves, but there were other indicators.

Alan warmed out his mount before boosting it over into the easy lope his father's people had favoured over all other gaits. No one in their right mind trotted a horse.

A loping horse could hold to his gait for miles. A running horse could rarely run for much more than a mile. A loping horse was like riding a rocking chair, and it could wear down two or three running horses, cover the same miles and arrive at its destination fresh.

The distance was not great and with good visibility and open country Alan Gardea had nothing to fear until he reached the town, and that did not prey on his mind, but it should have.

Someone had painted the name of the town on a large boulder beside the north–south roadway. Alan Gardea came into town from the west where there was no sign, but he had seen it many times in his life, and it never ceased making him smile.

The rock painting was very old and distinct, although faded. Its legend was in Spanish: '*El Ninguna Parte*', which, loosely translated, meant 'Nowhere', which was the English name most commonly used now.

Alan rode at a walk to the livery barn run by a tobacco-chewing, red-faced raffish man named Patrick Leary. When Leary saw him coming he hastened out front, and as Alan was dismounting, the livery man moved to take the reins as he said, 'Alan, you want to be real careful. There's some tough-looking lawmen in town. This morning they brought in a dead posseman who was ridin' with them ... The sheriff is pretty upset.'

Alan said, '*Gracias*,' and strode up the west side of the wide, dusty main thoroughfare as far as the *juzgado*, which he entered, and was immediately struck by the pleasant coolness provided by very thick adobe walls. At one time, a couple of generations earlier, Nowhere's jailhouse had been the headquarters of a Mexican *commandante*.

Burt Evans looked up from his desk, a troubled expression appeared and he rocked back in his chair until Gardea had been seated, then he said, 'That Wyoming lawman was in here a while ago mad enough to chew bullets and spit rust. That outlaw they was chasing, feller named Schilling, shot and killed one of his possemen. You don't know anything about that, do you?'

'How could I? I wasn't there.'

'Alan ... Schilling was riding a dun gelding with the Gardea brand on the left shoulder.'

For a moment as they gazed at each other the sheriff seemed more pained than angry. 'You had him at the ranch yesterday.'

'I told you, Burt, I'd talk to him, and if he didn't ring true I'd bring him to you in town.'

'He rang true? Alan, for Chris'sake you touched off a whirlwind of problems for me, an' for you.'

Alan stretched his legs. 'He wasn't a liar, Burt. If you'd heard his story you'd have done exactly what I did.'

'The hell I would have! Murder is shootin' someone

in the back. An unarmed man at that. Under the law I could lock you up as an accomplice. Comstock's sent a letter to the governor of Wyoming. Partner, why in hell didn't you just let him ride away on his own horse?'

'It couldn't have carried him thirty miles, Burt.'

Sheriff Evans leaned forward with both elbows atop the desk. Before he could speak Alan also said, 'At least one of them was spying on the yard last night. Otherwise they couldn't have caught him below the old goat-herder's *jacal.* They were careless; he heard them and was trying to make it to concealment when they ran at him. They killed the dun horse and shot him all to hell, and the one they brought back to town was the one Schilling shot off his horse.'

Sheriff Burns looked slightly hopeful. 'Schilling is dead?'

'Maybe by now he is, but when I left the yard he was still hanging on. That's why I came to town. To get Doc Emerson to go back with me.'

'Doc's over at the Gomez place deliverin' a baby.'

'That's not much of a ride and it's still early. I'll ride over and take him back with me.'

Sheriff Evans reddened. 'You ain't been payin' attention to what I said. Comstock is out for your scalp. For the scalp of anyone. He said when they went after the body they was fired on by *vaqueros* hidden around in the underbrush. He swore he saw you'n John Bristow among them.'

Alan shook his head slowly. 'He's a liar, Burt. He didn't see me. I wasn't out there when the fight started.'

'Alan, damn it, listen to me. That son of a bitch is as cold as ice and as hard as iron. He's goin' to kill you if he can.'

'Burt, I talked to him when he and his riders came into the yard. That's the only truck I've had with him.'

'To Clement Comstock, you hid his prisoner then helped him try to escape. He told me up in Wyoming they'd lynch you for that.'

'This is New Mexico, Burt. Six gunmen from Wyoming in our country aren't a drop in the bucket. If he tries to kill me, or anyone who rides for me, he'd better be a praying man.'

As Alan Gardea arose Sheriff Evans also came up to his feet. 'Don't go out to the Gomez place. Comstock's men will see you. They'll recognize you sure as hell, maybe follow you.' Burt Evans rolled his eyes and made almost a pleading gesture with both arms. 'You got me into trouble up to my ears, Alan. If you get killed there'll be hell to pay. Folks don't know Comstock yet, but when they do they're not goin' to like him. If you get killed a damned company of soldiers won't be able to prevent a wholesale lynching ... You see where you've put me?'

Alan stood with a hand on the door-latch gazing at Burt Evans. They had known each other for years, had been good friends. Alan hadn't considered the sheriff's position, but now he did. 'All right. I'll head back. After you promise me you'll send Doc Emerson to the ranch when he gets back to town.'

Sheriff Evans followed Alan Gardea outside, looked both ways and said, 'Be careful. Ride fast. I wouldn't bet a plugged *centavo* some of them haven't already recognized you.'

Alan returned to Leary's barn, got his horse and left town by the same westerly route he had used arriving there. The day was somewhat more advanced but visibility was still excellent.

He swore, something he did rarely. He should have

thought about Burt Evans's position in this damned mess those Wyoming lawmen had brought him.

He did not think it had been Charley Schilling who had brought him the trouble. He did not think about Charley at all until he had his yard in sight.

5 Silent Horses

There was one *vaquero* in the barn when Alan led his horse inside to be cared for. It was the same powerfully built rider Bristow had sent to make sure old Augustino Madrigal had been fed.

The yard was quiet except for garrulous birds in the trees and some foolish chickens squawking somewhere. As the *vaquero* took Alan's reins he smiled and said, 'John went to the marking ground.'

Alan nodded. When he had been a child his father had always left one or two men in the yard as a precaution. Evidently Bristow had learned that years back and had done it this time.

Juan was pock-marked, strong as oak and fearless. Like Bristow and the other riders, he was loyal and protective. His size and temper made it unlikely anyone who was sober would make derogatory remarks in his presence.

Alan crossed to the main house, entered and detected the smell of something he had to try to place. Carbolic acid. He went to Schilling's bedroom, found his mother there feeding the wounded man, and they both looked up as he appeared in the doorway.

Dorotea faintly frowned. 'Doctor Emerson?'

'He was delivering a baby at the Gomez ranch. Burt Evans said he'd send him along as soon as he found him.' Alan nodded in the direction of the man in the bed. 'How is he?' he asked in Spanish and got an answer from his mother in English.

'Better. He's a healthy, strong man.'

Dorotea turned back to feeding her patient and Alan returned to the *sala*, the main parlour, dropped into a chair and was still sitting there when Maria came along, unsmiling and direct.

'Where is the doctor, *niño*?'

'He'll be along,' Alan replied and looked up at the heavy, dark woman. 'My mother is feeding him.'

Maria's black eyes remained fixed on Alan. 'Someone had to.'

'Why not you, Maria?'

'... Because she wanted to,' the dark woman said, looking steadily at Dorotea's son. They gazed at one another for a long moment before the *mestizo* woman left the room.

When the riders returned in late afternoon John Bristow was in a better mood; the cattle had scarcely drifted at all. He asked about the doctor, Alan replied and John said, 'Well, maybe tomorrow we can start at the marking ground,' and walked in the direction of his *jacal*.

Doctor Emerson arrived just short of sundown. He was an untidy, rumpled, large man who wore matching coat and britches and was addicted to little crooked Mexican cigars.

When he climbed down from his top-buggy and left the old thousand-pound mare who pulled it standing at the tie-rack, he didn't bother to drop the tether-weight. The mare had been making rounds with Doctor Emerson for nine years. Wherever he left her she remained rooted until he returned. They were both somewhat overweight. They were also both very pragmatic.

Alan admitted Doctor Emerson at the massive oaken door and wordlessly took him to Charley Schilling's room, then stood aside and watched.

Emerson completed his examination under the steady gaze of his patient, straightened and faced Alan as he gruffly said, 'When did it happen?'

'Night before last.'

Doctor Emerson turned back toward the bed, ignored the stare of the injured man and gave his opinion. 'Well; if he'd lost too much blood he'd be dead by now.' He bent to begin re-bandaging the wounds with rolls of cloth from his black satchel. 'But he'll be flat on his back for quite a while. The shoulder injury will heal – leave a scar but what the hell ... The other wound ... Who takes care of him, Alan?'

'My mother.'

'Ah; that's good. Over the years I've seen her do small miracles. Is she handy?'

Alan went to find his mother, and bring her back to the room where Doctor Emerson gallantly kissed her hand, then became very brisk. He spoke Spanish, but never unless he had to. He spoke to the handsome woman in English. Very plain English, because that was the way he always spoke.

'*Señora*, you know what the danger is in cases like this?'

'Infection?'

'Yes. Infection and catching something that could turn into pneumonia.' Emerson looked dispassionately at Charley Schilling. 'He's a good physical specimen; unless there are complications he'll recover. In time, *Señora.* In time. I've never seen even a man as strong as this one, recover from the kinds of injuries he has very quickly.'

Dorotea's gaze drifted to Charley Schilling. 'There will be no need for a miracle, Doctor.'

Alan was watching his mother when she made that remark. He glanced toward the bed. Charley Schilling was looking steadily back at her.

Doctor Emerson opened his satchel wide, removed two bottles and handed them to Alan's mother. 'When you change bandages put some of this in the wash-water. The other is laudanum. Only for very bad pain. You understand?'

Dorotea nodded. 'I appreciate you coming,' she told the big rumpled man as he turned to snap his satchel closed. As he turned, satchel in hand he said, 'One dollar.'

Dorotea and Doctor Emerson left the room together.

Alan swung a chair around and straddled it. He told the injured man what the sheriff had said without mentioning the part about Schilling – and Alan Gardea – putting Burt Evans in an unenviable position.

Charley's response was about the same as everything he had said even before they'd brought him to the yard. 'Mister Gardea, you should have left me down yonder with the old man.'

Alan replied dryly, 'We brought the old man back too. Comstock might try to wring his neck until he told him my riders and I were down there and hauled you back.'

Charley Schilling's gaze rolled ceilingward, then back to Gardea. 'I made a gawddamned mess of it. Got you, the old man and most likely everyone else into a mess you got no hand in.'

'We've got a hand in it now, Charley.'

'In a few days I'll be able to sit a saddle.'

'You heard what the doctor said.'

'Mister Gardea, the longer I stay here the rougher things are goin' to get for you ...'

'Charley, my name is Alan. Alan Gardea. You're stuck here for a long while. Just about everyone else calls me Alan. You might as well too ... Tell me something, Charley, how did you manage to hit that son of a bitch right through the brisket in darkness?'

It required a moment for Schilling to understand the implication behind the question. Eventually he said, 'You have line camps down here?'

Alan shook his head.

'Maybe you know what it's like bein' stuck in a line camp to stop drift and pull hung-up calves and keep sore-footed bulls from spendin' the summer in mudholes ... It's a lonely life. Some fellers read books, some break a horse or two. I bought extra ammunition and practised with guns.'

Alan looked steadily at the other man. 'Seeing that man you killed over your gunsights as you practised?'

Charley smiled a little. 'You figure things, don't you? That's exactly what I did.'

'Got pretty good with guns, did you?'

'Maybe a tad better than average. I had a reason. Alan, there are some cartwheels in my pants pocket. Take one to your mother to pay for the doctor.'

Alan arose and spun the chair back where it had been but did not approach the pile of bloody clothing on a little bench as he said, 'I don't like to answer personal questions. I guess you don't either.'

Charley said, 'Shoot. What is it?'

'How old are you?'

'Thirty-five. Be thirty-six in a couple of months.'

'You ever been married, Charley?'

Schilling's face smoothed out in surprise. 'Nope, never have. I had other things to think about.'

Alan turned in the doorway for his final remark. 'Those things have been taken care of.'

Charley Schilling's gaze remained on the empty doorway long after Alan Gardea had departed. Then he slept. When he awakened the formidable dark woman named Maria was placing a large basin of hot water on the table. She had two towels draped over one arm. When she turned, saw the steady gaze of the wounded man, she said, 'First, let me tell you, *gringo*, I've buried two husbands. You have nothing that can surprise me. Roll over, I'll start on your back.'

Charley obeyed and as the dark *mestizo* woman began bathing him she said, 'I won't get the bandages wet unless you move ... Where is your family?'

Charley replied curtly. 'I don't have a family.'

'No brothers or sisters, no wife?'

'No.'

Maria concentrated on her work for a while. She only spoke again when she had Schilling lie on his back. As she started scrubbing his chest, very gently, she said, 'You will get well.'

Charley looked at her in silence. Maria was one of those formidable women who made men wary even when they knew her. More wary when they didn't.

She paused to look him in the face. 'How old are you, *Señor*?'

He replied, as he usually answered questions, forthrightly. 'Coming up to thirty-six. Mind if I ask you a question?'

'No,' Maria replied, holding the soapy scrub cloth poised.

'That's the second time today someone's asked me that. Is age important, down here in New Mexico?'

Maria went to work with the wet cloth. 'Alan asked you?'

'Yes.'

Maria ducked her head and scrubbed for a few moments before speaking again. 'No. In New Mexico age isn't important.'

'You are just curious?'

'Yes. Now look at the ceiling if you want to.'

Charley endured the bath but as Maria was picking up the soggy towels and the basin he had another question for her. 'How old is Alan?'

'Thirty-five,' Maria replied and left the room with her basin.

Charley lay a long while, puzzled and curious. Before falling asleep again he decided New Mexicans were an odd bunch.

One of the riders was down in front of the barn talking to John Bristow when Alan crossed the yard. The rider abruptly broke off the discussion and led his horse into the barn to be off-saddled and looked after.

John leaned on the tie-rack studying the immense sweep of northward range when Alan came up and said, 'How did it go at the marking ground today?'

John answered indifferently. 'Well enough. We worked through eighty-eight steer calves and marked altogether one hundred and eleven by count ... Alan?'

'Yes.'

'I left him out there to drag in more wood for the branding fire. He was up near Escalante Canyon and saw three men settin' their horses half-hid in the rocks.'

Alan met the steady gaze of his rangeboss. 'Did he get a good look at them?'

'No. All he saw was three fellers watchin' him from among the rocks. He didn't have his sidearm so he acted like he was just after the wood, roped some snags, dragged them back, left 'em and came home.'

John regarded the younger man as Alan leaned, looked around and eventually said, 'Did you ever hear the old Mex saying that the way to stop fire is to throw the first bucket of water?'

Bristow nodded without speaking until Alan said a little more. 'Maybe if we caught some of them, John …'

Bristow nodded again without speaking until he'd shifted position a little. 'They're *coyote*, Alan.'

Gardea made a hard little smile. 'This is our country, John. We know a little about that too.'

'Tonight?'

Alan sighed. 'I guess so. If they're out there they'll hear you coming. If they're not out there you could be in position if they return.'

The rangeboss shrugged. 'They won't hear anything. I'll take Juan and Fred Olmstead.'

As the rangeboss headed for his little mud house Alan Gardea leaned and watched him. Everyone lately, including Charley Schilling, had warned him. Not that he particularly had to be warned. The look on the face and in the eyes of that deputy from Wyoming had been warning enough.

He swore softly in Spanish. They did not need distractions right now, with cattle to be worked, but he'd never heard it said that trouble waited until someone was prepared for it.

He could smell cooking fires, which reminded him he was hungry so he re-crossed the yard and entered the patio. His mother was sitting out there in tree shade and smiled up at him. He repeated Bristow's tally of worked calves and she said, 'No losses. We've had a couple of good years ... What are you looking so glum about?'

Alan smiled. 'I'm hungry.'

They entered the house together and as Alan went to clean up his mother went to the back of the house where Charley Schilling was softly snoring. She stood a moment in the doorway speculating about something that had surfaced twice today. How old was he?

Instinct offered a fair guess but something else inclined her to believe he should be older.

When she went to the dining-room Maria was already feeding her son. The dark woman shot her mistress a worried look and padded into the kitchen for more food.

After dark, two residents of the main house went to bed but not to sleep for a long while, altogether different thoughts churning in their minds.

Alan did not hear riders leave the yard, which he probably would not have heard anyway, but his thoughts rode with them. Eventually there would be a show-down with the men from Wyoming. He did not fear it; he only wished it could have waited until they were through working the cattle.

In the morning when he went down to saddle a horse he stood a long while studying the ground where three shod horses had made marks which overlaid all the previous marks. He was still standing there looking down when an old *vaquero* named Sancho Pedregal came along. Pedregal was old; he had ridden for the ranch since his youth. Now, he did a few chores, hauled wood when he felt like it, and dozed in the shade.

He stopped, nodded to the *patrón*, followed Alan's gaze, looked closer and finally said, 'Not in fifteen years have I seen that, *Señor*. In your father's time we did it. Not often, only when your father knew it would be necessary.' The old man leaned down and squinted, blew out a slow breath as he straightened up and said, 'But we used soft cowhide. Those – they wrapped the horses' feet in sacking.'

Alan nodded. 'Just as quiet, Sancho.'

The old *vaquero* was not sure of that. 'Not if they have to ride very far, *Patrón*, steel shoes will chew through sacking. It would have been better if they'd used cowhide. Then they could ride much farther ... I rode many times in the night with your father when we stalked *Indios*. Sometimes for many miles.' The old man stopped talking, considered the cumbersome-looking big flat tracks, and said, 'Did you know, *Patrón*?'

'Yes.'

'Ah. that's why there was no smoke coming from the *mayordomo*'s house this morning ... And the house of Juan Aguilar ... *Indios*? No, there haven't been *Indios* for years.'

Alan went on through the barn to catch a horse in the big circular corral out back. When he led it inside to be saddled the old *vaquero* was gone.

Word would spread; it always did among the riders, the women, and inevitably it would reach Maria at the *hacienda*.

As Alan led his horse outside to be mounted he glanced in the direction of the patio before mounting. As he was reining away he sighed again. Maria Escobar was like a weather vane. She detected the first hint of gossip and Alan had been present any number of times when she had taken the stories to his mother.

Last night he just hadn't had the heart to tell her about the plan he and John Bristow had hatched. As he rode through dazzling autumn sunshine with heat on his back, he had no illusions about his mother not knowing when he returned.

Escalante Canyon was not much of a ride to anyone who had traversed the distance a hundred times. He had cattle in sight before he saw the rocky strip of ground near the canyon's lip. Closer still, three Gardea riders were working cattle through, but instead of two ropers on horseback this morning, there was one, and instead of two men to roughneck the bawling calves to the fire, there was one man. The third was chopping wood for the branding fire.

When he came up, the sweating, rumpled men grinned and went on about their work. Alan draped his catch-rope around the horn and rode over to where the wet cows were bawling their heads off every time a calf squalled as the hot iron was applied.

He roped a calf and dragged it to the men. They flung off his rope, made quick wraps with their pigging strings and Alan turned back for another calf.

It was the kind of bruising, sweaty work that made time pass quickly. The sun was directly overhead before anyone knew it. They freed the last calf to go high-tailing it back to some wet cow, removed their gloves, beat off dust, which flew, and ignored the blood which was drying on their clothing.

Alan hobbled his horse and joined them in meagre shade for a noon meal. Very little was said, except good-natured jibes at the roper who missed an occasional catch, or the castrating and ear-marking man who swore he always got a too-hot iron from the fire-tender.

They watched Alan askance. They knew Bristow and the other two men of the full complement had not been in the yard when they'd trooped down for their animals. It had been still a little dark so they hadn't seen the tracks of muffled hooves. But they 'felt' something was happening and would not have asked questions if they'd been dragged behind wild horses.

They tanked up from canteens and went back to work, more slowly than when they'd first arrived at the marking ground. Regardless of how experienced a man was at dumping fighting bundles of a hundred-and-fifty pounds to be lashed and worked, it was not possible to do this kind of work without getting kicked, run over and knocked flat by some orry-eyed old mammy cow who charged at the bawling of her calf.

They were hard, tough men. If they hadn't been when they'd first started out, they became that way within a short time, or they quit and hunted up a town where making a living was less bruising and much less dangerous.

Alan spelled off one of the drag-men. He busted calves, lashed them and ear-marked them as the other man attended to the castration of bull calves, or, if it was a heifer calf, Alan helped the fire-tender split wood.

The afternoon passed almost as swiftly as the morning had. Occasionally Alan would stand erect looking in the direction of Escalante Canyon, saw nothing, and couldn't have heard cannon-fire because of the deafening racket slobbering, fretting mammy cows made.

When they were ready to call it quits for the day a hard-eyed rider approached Alan and said, 'You been lookin' out yonder pretty often. If you want, couple of us can ride over there.'

Alan slapped the man on the shoulder and went to get his horse for the ride home. The hard-eyed cowboy went among his companions and spoke in incredibly bad Spanish for the benefit of one of the Mexican riders who knew very little English.

'I can smell trouble, friends. The boss is worried. Let's get back and catch Juan Bristow when he comes back. A man can't be of help if he doesn't know what in hell is exactly going forward, can he?'

Of course they knew some of it; they'd chased off those riders down near the old man's *jacal.* They wanted to know more but would not ask.

6 Alan Gardea's Plan

It was close to sundown when John Bristow came to the patio. He hadn't eaten, was rumpled and dusty-looking and did not smile when the *mestizo* maid darted to find Alan and send him to the patio.

Being a direct individual John spoke curtly the moment Alan arrived. 'We got one. He's chained in the barn. We scouted around. I think he was the only one. But sure as hell that big ox with the whiskers will miss this one.'

They crossed toward the barn with fragrant cooking fires sending pale smoke from the *jacals.* The man chained to a supporting big log on the south side of the barn was thin and wiry. Alan remembered his face from the only time all of the Wyoming posse-riders had been in the yard.

It was perhaps to the posseman's credit that he gave Alan and John look for look. Not quite in defiance, but certainly without fear.

Alan asked the man his name. The answer was cold. 'John Smith.'

The rangeboss, grim on the ride back to the yard with the prisoner, leaned and swung the fist holding his riding gloves. It was more a slap than a strike, but the chained man's head snapped. Bristow leaned slightly from the waist. 'Answer when you're spoken to or I'll get that big Mexican who tackled you off the horse to come back.'

The prisoner's face reddened; he glared at the rangeboss. 'Turn me loose, you son of a bitch, an' give me back my gun an' we'll see ...'

Bristow's second blow was with a bony fist. A flung-back thin streak of blood showed where the man's head had turned swiftly. He blinked several times, then showed ferocity in his regard of the rangeboss.

He could not raise a hand to his split lip so he spat before speaking again. 'Let me tell you something, mister. Deputy Comstock's already sent a letter to the governor of Wyoming. You think he won't contact the governor of this damned greaser country? He'll ask for soldiers to be sent down here to make the law work.'

Alan regarded the posse-rider. He was a hard, stubborn man, obviously unafraid although in his position most men would have been. Alan spoke quietly. 'Fetch him something to eat, John,' and after the rangeboss had turned angrily away Alan squatted so that their eyes were on the same level and addressed the prisoner.

'You don't know this – greaser – country. Two things you ought to know. Be very careful when you say "greaser". It probably doesn't mean much to you, but down here they'll kill you for saying it. The other thing is that most of the ranchers around here are related. Blue-eyed or brown-eyed. If men like you come here looking for trouble, you'll get a hell of a surprise ... Now, let's try again: what is your name?'

The wiry, weathered man's grey eyes neither blinked nor left Alan Gardea's face. He had seen, and heard, Gardea before. One thing impressed men such as he, and that was calm, fearless speech. He said, 'Willard Bowman, an' you're Alan Gardea ... You or someone who works for you shot one of our riders. Mister, that was a mistake. You don't know Clem Comstock.'

Alan thinly smiled. 'Willard, I'll give you some advice. Leave. Go back where you came from. Go anywhere but don't let Deputy Comstock get you killed.'

The chained man showed no fear. 'We got the law, Mister Gardea.'

'Not down here you haven't. Get on your horse and don't look back. Unless you want to stay down here permanently. What were you watching for when my rangeboss caught you?'

'Your rangeboss didn't even come out of the rocks until after that big greaser –'

'Willard, I told you. His name is Juan. If he heard you call him that he'd strangle you.'

'– until Juan snuck up behind me like an In'ian, and launched himself over the rock right atop me.'

'All right. What were you doing out there?'

'Watchin' things.'

'Why?'

'... We know you got that outlaw somewhere around.'

Alan paused as John Bristow returned with a platter of *entamotados*, put it on the ground and knelt to free the prisoner's arms. Willard Bowman regarded the platter with a faint scowl. 'What the hell is that? We heard you folks eat dog an' goats an –'

Bristow snapped. 'It's beef. You can starve for all I care.'

The prisoner ignored Bristow and looked up at Alan. 'You better turn me loose. When I don't get back to that Mex town with the measly sheriff, Mister Comstock'll be after you like the devil after a crippled saint.'

Alan shrugged. 'He'll hear about what happened if we turn you loose. Eat.'

'I ain't as hungry as I'm thirsty.'

Bristow yanked the man's hat off and went out back to fill it from the trough and bring it back. Willard Bowman drank it half-empty, the other half leaked on to the ground.

Bowman felt his split lip, which had stopped bleeding and was swelling. He shot a venomous glare at the rangeboss as Alan said, 'Eat or we'll chain you up again on an empty gut.'

Bowman ate, tentatively at first, then like a bitch wolf. When he had finished the rangeboss knelt, re-chained him and stood up smiling. 'That's two, cowboy. There's only four left countin' that big ox with the whiskers.'

Bowman remained undaunted. 'Rangeboss, you don't know ... Clem Comstock ain't even begun yet.'

Alan and John Bristow returned to the yard. John shook his head but said nothing. Alan leaned on the tie-rack. There might be a way to conclude this affair quickly. He leaned in thought and eventually said, 'He'll come out here – with what's left of his posse. If we knew when, we could end this once and for all.'

John squinted, tipped down his hat and blew out a rough breath. 'What worries me was that them bastards was out near the markin' ground to wait until we was gone, then maybe stampede the cattle to hell an' gone.'

That notion had not occurred to Alan Gardea. After a little thought he shook his head. 'They're after Charley Schilling. They know he's out here.'

'Then they'll come.'

Alan straightened up off the tie-rack gazing in the direction of the main house. As he started away he said, 'Keep the riders around in the morning.'

'Why?'

'I have an idea, John. If it works we'd ought to be able to get back to the cattle maybe day after tomorrow ... Send Alf Olmstead over to the main house in a little while. Not right away; in half an hour.'

John Bristow watched his employer cross the yard and disappear beyond the patio's gateless opening in the wall, then spat and considered returning to the barn, but in the end when he left the tie-rack he headed toward his *jacal*.

It was a pleasant, dying day with scarcely even a hint that autumn was on the land, which meant it should have been cooler this close to sundown.

Alan went through to Charley Schilling's room and was not surprised to find his mother there. He was not surprised but he was concerned.

She picked up a plate and cup, smiled at her son and departed. Alan and Charley regarded each other.

Charley said, 'She's a real lady,' and Alan nodded as he went to the chair his mother had vacated.

'We caught one of Comstock's riders. He's chained in the barn. Does the name Willard Bowman mean anything to you?'

'No. Is that his name?'

'Yes … Charley, I have a wild-hair of an idea. I need your help.'

'You got it, Mister Gardea.'

'… Alan, remember. Alan.'

'What's the idea?'

'They know you're here. They don't know you're in the main house, but sure as hell Comstock'll figure that possibility. After talking to our prisoner I don't believe there's any way to avoid shooting. I don't want them near this house, not with my mother here and the others.'

Alan smiled slightly at the bewildered look he was getting from the wounded man. 'I have a rider named Alfred Olmstead built like you, the same height, and after sundown with no one to see his face clearly …' Alan nodded to the little bench where Charley Schilling's clothes had been. 'Maria take them away to be washed?'

'Your mother did.'

Alan considered that and pushed the implication aside as he arose from the chair. 'I'll find them.'

He was approaching the door when Schilling said, 'I could do it. They might see your rider's face and know he wasn't …'

'You *can't* do it, Charley.'

'I feel a hundred per cent better. I'll ride slow an' be real careful.'

Alan's gaze clouded with annoyance. 'And what would you do if it came to a fight? Hell, Charley, I don't care how you feel, you stay in that bed. Don't add to my other worries. All right?'

Schilling nodded curtly and Alan went out to the *sala* where John Bristow was waiting, hat in hand, and Maria was hovering like an aggravated vulture. John jerked his head. Alf Olmstead was on the bench in the patio. Before closing the massive oaken door Alan turned and said, 'Maria, where are Schilling's clothes?'

'Washed and ironed. *Niño*, you can't let him leave that bed.'

Alan smiled at the thick, dark woman. 'He's not going to leave the bed. Bring his clothes to me out here.'

Alf Olmstead was a quiet, even-tempered man, and he was no fool. When Maria brought the clothing, folded, clean and pressed, Olmstead looked from the clothing to Alan Gardea.

The rangeboss explained and Olmstead remained impassive for a few moments, then shrugged, something all the *gringo* riders had picked up from the *vaqueros*. 'An' suppose they're all out there, John?'

'I'll dog after you.'

Alan nodded. 'We both will. What you can do if they appear is turn back, make a run for it. You'll be riding Schilling's horse. If they don't recognize the clothing they will know the horse. They trailed it long enough.'

Olmstead nodded slowly, clearly speculating on the dangers. In the end he grinned at Alan. 'Just remember the feller on the first runnin' horse you see is me.'

He and John Bristow left the patio with Alf Olmstead carrying Charley Schilling's clothes. Alan watched them briefly then turned – and was facing his mother. Behind her was the ever-present, unsmiling very dark woman.

Dorotea said, 'He could get killed, Alan.'

'That could happen if he got bucked off in the rocks. John and I'll be back a ways.' Alan went toward his mother. 'So far it's been all Comstock's doings. Now it's our turn. Mother, those men are holding up everything we should be doing. I want this ended one way or the other.'

'Alan, they are bad men.'

Dorotea's son smiled a little. 'Yes. John and I will take the man we have chained in the barn. If it looks bad we'll turn him loose to head off his friends.'

'Alan ...!'

'*Madre mía*,' he said in Spanish, 'be tranquil. It will be all right.'

Maria spoke from behind Alan's mother. 'Take Juan Aguilar. Some of the others.' She had decided after listening to the exchange between Dorotea and her son – whom Maria knew very well – that Alan's mind was made up.

He smiled at the dark, heavy woman, and told her in Spanish she worried too much. Her reply to that was a derisive snort unaccompanied by any words.

Alan left them in the doorway, crossed the yard and entered the barn as John Bristow was leading Charley Schilling's horse inside. Alan appraised the animal from the viewpoint of a lifelong horseman when Bristow made the horse fast as he said, 'Not quite as good as new but damned close to it. He'll make out all right. Alf's in his *jacal* trying on the clothes.' John went after a rice-straw brush and cuffing comb. 'Tamale telegraph's been busy. Everyone knows what's goin' on. At least they know something is.'

Alan shrugged about that. He had learned at a very early age the best way to keep a secret in the yard was to tell it first.

Alf Olmstead entered the barn from out back. If it had been darker neither Alan nor his rangeboss would have been able to tell him from the man in bed at the main house.

Whether the disguise would work or not was anyone's guess. Unless the posse-riders had seen Charley Schilling before he had shot it out with them down by the old man's *jacal*, they might not recognize the clothing. Maybe they'd had a good sighting before the shoot-out, although that too was problematical, but they surely knew his horse.

Olmstead said, 'Juan wants to go.'

Bristow looked at Alan for the reply to that. He may have liked the idea but the decision belonged to the *patrón*.

Alan asked if Alf was worried. Olmstead made a crooked small smile when he replied. 'A man'd have to be a damned idiot not to be. But I ain't scairt if that's what you mean.'

Alan returned to the doorless wide barn opening and looked easterly where the land was without decent shelter. When John approached, leaving Alf to rig out the Schilling horse, Alan said, 'If we give the devil his due, John, then we got to figure they're watching the yard.'

John was not particularly worried because Alf would not leave until dusk with Alan and John trailing him. He mentioned the prisoner and they walked back where Willard Bowman had been enormously curious about something that was obviously part of some plan. Alan asked the captive if he'd been fed and got a nod as Bowman jutted his chin in the direction of Olmstead and the horse. 'What's that all about?'

Alan countered with a question. 'Do you recognize the horse?'

'Ought to, mister, we seen him up pretty close the last day or two before you fellers butted in.'

Alan and John Bristow exchanged a look. The rangeboss said, 'How'd you like to meet your friends?'

The rangeboss could have handed Willard Bowman a hatful of gold and the wiry, fearless man would have looked askance. He did not like John Bristow, and during his time alone had made up his mind that at the first opportunity he would kill him. Now, he looked blankly at the rangeboss, wary and suspicious.

'You goin' to set me loose?'

John shook his head slowly. 'Not quite. The feller saddling Schilling's horse is goin' to ride toward town. You'n Alan and I'll shag him back a ways so when your watcher out there hightails it to fetch Comstock to catch the feller dressed like Schilling an' ridin' his horse, we can meet them.'

Bowman's mouth hung open. He continued to regard the rangeboss for a long time before speaking. 'You're goin' to get that cowboy killed.'

Bristow gazed at the chained man. 'That'll mean they'll be out there, don't it?'

Instead of replying to Bristow the captive looked at Alan Gardea. 'What's that supposed to prove?'

'That Charley Schilling is heading out of the country.'

'But we seen him go down on that dun horse.'

'And you saw him fire back and kill one of your riders.'

'Mister, we shot him. We saw him flop. If you got

him hid out somewhere one thing Clem an' the others know, is that Schilling most likely can't set a horse.'

Alan did not disagree, he mildly said, 'Most likely he can't sit a horse. But maybe he can too. No one else would ride Schilling's horse.'

Bowman raised his voice in the direction of the man looping the *latigo* as he finished rigging out Charley Schilling's animal. 'Hey, cowboy, these fellers are crazy. They're to get you killed.'

Olmstead answered without facing around. 'No one dies a minute before, or a minute later, than their time.'

Bowman faintly frowned at Olmstead's back. 'If you let them talk you into this you're as crazy as they are.'

Bristow leaned down to unchain Willard Bowman, and as the captive arose stiffly John poked him in the middle of the chest with a stiff finger. 'Don't do anything silly, mister. You ride between me'n Alan. You so much as look like you're goin' to yell or make a run for it and I'll blow your damned head off.'

Bowman met Bristow's menacing gaze without flinching. 'I know your name. It's Bristow. One day I'll come lookin' for you.'

Alan headed off his rangeboss's forming reply by sending John out back for another horse and the moment the rangeboss was out of sight Alan quietly said, 'Willard, you won't have to come looking for him. Now then, remember what he told you; you'll ride between us.'

'Why? What the hell is it goin' to prove for you to take me along?'

'Maybe we'll turn you loose.'

Bowman stared perplexedly at Gardea. 'Turn me loose? Mister, if Deputy Comstock meets you out there with the riders he's got left, you won't have to set me loose, I'll ride over your carcasses.'

'Who is the man who's been spying on the yard today?'

'Hell I don't know.'

'But he's out there.'

Bowman looked over where Alf Olmstead was standing hip-shot beside Schilling's horse. When he faced Alan again he said, 'Find that out for yourself.'

Alan nodded. It was hard not to respect Willard Bowman's toughness. Even his swollen split lip and the knowledge that they could kill him any time they wanted to, which both combined had to convince Bowman his life was in the balance, did not deter his defiance. Alan said, 'If you're ever out of work and need a job, look me up.'

Bowman faintly scowled. Alan nodded. 'I mean it. If you're down here long enough you'll learn that – greasers – put a high value on loyalty.'

'I didn't say you was a greaser, mister.'

Alan almost smiled. 'That's good. Otherwise I'd kill you.' He left the posse-rider staring after him as he went over where John Bristow was tying a horse. Willard Bowman shook his head.

After John saddled and bridled the horse Bowman was to ride he went up to the wide front entrance to the barn, studied the sky, the shadowing land and walked back. Alf Olmstead said, 'About time, John?'

The rangeboss nodded and turned to Alan. 'I'll bring in our horses.'

Olmstead led his animal out front to be mounted, took a hasty look around then swung up over leather and walked his mount out of the yard.

It was not quite dusk. It was the brief in-between time which did not linger long when there was no daylight and visibility was not as limited as it would be an hour from now.

7 A Crisis

Bristow said, 'Alan, I thought all the riders would go with us.'

Gardea's response indicated there had been more to his scheme than a confrontation. 'No. If Comstock gets around us, he'll head for the yard looking for Schilling.'

The rangeboss did not hesitate. 'I'll tell Juan to pass the word around.'

Alan tested the cincha on the horse he would ride, found it snug without being tight, and led the animal up where the interior shadows almost ended as he watched Alf Olmstead, who was riding toward Nowhere following the route horsemen from the Gardea compound had taken for over a hundred years.

When John returned Alan turned to mount his horse inside the barn so he would still be in shadows if the spy out yonder hadn't already seen 'Charley Schilling' riding eastward.

Bristow had a carbine in a saddle boot. When he mounted he looked grim. Alan waited until Alf Olmstead was barely discernible in the soft, fading pre-dusk, then rode out of the barn with his rangeboss behind him.

If the season had not been so advanced, daylight and its residual pre-twilight period would have lingered until about nine o'clock. As it was Alan estimated the period of pre-dusk light might endure until somewhat earlier, which meant his *vaquero* up ahead would be visible to Alan and John Bristow for perhaps another hour or slightly less.

He could have closed the distance but didn't, for the reason that if Comstock got out here in time to see Alf Olmstead, if he and John Bristow were much closer Comstock would also see them, the exact thing Alan did not want.

John rode in silence. Up until Alan had told him in the barn the entire riding crew would not be along, he had derived grim satisfaction from the notion that the Gardea riders would outnumber the Comstock riders, and if that had been the case there would have been little to worry about.

The odds, in John Bristow's opinion, were something it was better not to dwell on, even assuming he and Alan could surprise the posse-riders.

Alan turned once to look at his companion, then sat forward without speaking. Nothing was said between them until it became a little difficult to maintain the distance and still make out the man riding the Schilling horse up ahead.

Bristow stood in his stirrups, then sat down. 'It should happen directly,' he told Gardea. 'Their spy's had enough time to reach town and head back with 'em.'

Alan did not quite agree; they'd only been riding for half an hour, but he shrugged and mentioned something else. 'If we can knock Comstock off his horse maybe his hired possemen'll begin to wonder. They had one killed and for all they know our friend here is dead too.'

Willard Bowman, quiet as a stone up until now, was uneasy. He had been doing some basic arithmetic as John Bristow had done, and believed as John believed, that if Comstock was coming, it would not be long before Gardea's plan either blew up in his face, or resulted in an ambush from which Deputy Comstock and his companions might not ride away. He surreptitiously watched the man on each side of him. Alan Gardea worried him less than did the rangeboss whose firepower would be greater with that Winchester under his *rosadero*.

Darkness would be Alf's ally providing he could cover enough distance in a run before Bristow could un-ship that Winchester.

Bowman had gauged the merit of the Gardea horse he was on. It was a run-of-the-mill using animal with nothing outstanding about it, which probably meant that while he might be able to jump it out when he made his dash, it would not be as fast as a more breedy animal would be. And that meant it would be unable to get him clear before the rangeboss went into action with his saddlegun.

Alan turned to Bowman. 'Nice night.'

The Wyomingite neither replied nor looked around.

John Bristow reined close. 'I told you, when someone speaks to you, you son of a bitch, you answer.'

Bowman sullenly said, 'Yeah, beautiful night. Enjoy it, Mister Gardea.'

The implication was not lost on either of his companions but Bristow was already letting the distance between them widen as he frowned into the tricky light up ahead. It was Alan using the same quiet, calm tone of voice who said, 'You too, *amigo*. Where we go, you go.'

Half a mile further along Willard Bowman gave the first indication that his trouble had been gnawing at him since his capture. He said, 'Why in hell didn't you just ride to that roominghouse in town? They wouldn't have expected that.'

'The sheriff is a friend of mine,' Alan replied. 'I wouldn't do something that would put him between a rock and a hard place. Out here, where I own the land and noise won't reach town, is better.'

'Mister Gardea, you don't know what you two are goin' up against. Clem Comstock for all his size, is one of the deadliest men with a handgun I ever knew. Those fellers ridin' with him was hired because they got reputations as gunfighters.'

Bristow regarded Bowman. 'You too?'

The prisoner ignored John. Now that he was committed to trying to reason with, or frighten, Alan Gardea, he addressed him again.

'There's four. You're two. They're professional shooters. You're ranchers. What I couldn't figure out was why you didn't just hand Schilling over. He ain't nothin' to you, an' he sure as hell ain't worth gettin' killed over.'

Alan drew rein. Alf was plainly visible up ahead; he and his companions had closed the distance too fast. As they all watched the Schilling horse begin to dim-out up ahead, Alan replied to Bowman.

'It's the idea of a band of manhunters running a man to ground so they could kill him … On a worn-out horse, in a country strange to him. Without a chance of getting clear. Sort of like shooting a cougar stalking a baby calf. Something like that, eh John?'

Bristow's reply was brusque. 'Yeah. Something like that.'

Bowman was frowning when he said, 'The son of a bitch is a murderer. You folks down here like murderers?'

'No one likes murderers,' replied Gardea. 'And it's too bad he hated that man badly enough to shoot him in the back. But, Willard, if a man leaves it up to the Bible's statement that vengeance is mine saith the Lord, and I will repay, a feller like the one Schilling killed hurt a lot of other folks and would have continued to hurt them. Back-shooting isn't right, but sometimes if it's the only way to kill a man like Foster ...' Alan shrugged and Willard Bowman continued to look at him right up until John Bristow swung to the ground, knelt with his ear to the earth, arose, dusted off and swung back into the saddle before saying, 'Well, there's someone up ahead. It ain't just Alf. An' it don't have to be the posse-riders, but right now, this evenin', I can't imagine it bein' anyone else.'

They eased ahead at a dead walk. Alf Olmstead was now lost in the deepening gloom. Both Gardea and Bristow pulled loose the tie-down thongs which held their sixguns in holsters.

Willard Bowman was sweating and it wasn't that warm a night. He would be the only mounted unarmed man. If there was a fight he would be helpless.

He finally said, 'I go free after this is over?' and when Alan inclined his head the worried posseman said, 'I been on other hunts with Clem Comstock. He ain't goin' to run straight at the feller on Schilling's horse, he'll split 'em up and come at him from both sides.'

Alan halted, looked at John Bristow until the rangeman spoke. 'Be better if we had the whole crew, but we don't have so I expect we'd ought to ride northward a ways and with some luck catch the two Comstock'll send over in that direction.'

Bowman sat like a stone listening. When Alan reined to his left to follow out Bristow's suggestion, Bowman did not even hesitate. Like it or not, he was on the side he'd have given anything not to be on, but, being in that position, his only thought was to survive.

'You should've brought a saddlegun,' he told Alan, and got no response.

Without warning a man's high shout carried down through the dusk. Alan and Bristow stopped dead still. Bowman said, 'Who in hell was that?'

'Comstock.'

'Naw. When he bellers it sounds like a ruttin' bull.'

Bristow spoke softly. 'One of the others?'

Bowman shook his head. 'Don't no one make that kind of noise when they're ridin' with Comstock. That's his law when we're on a hunt. Not a damned sound.'

They sat near a flourishing stand of manzanita, its dollar-round pale leaves and bright red trunks notable now not for their unique colouring as much as for their protective shelter if it was needed.

Bristow dismounted to put his ear to the ground again and this time when he arose he shook his head. 'Nothing. Not any movement.' As John swung back into his saddle he also said, 'Whoever that hollerer was he stopped everything dead still, includin' Alf.'

There was a long moment of indecision; Alan had anticipated nothing like this turn of events. John Bristow sat wearing a puzzled scowl. It was Willard Bowman who came up with a possible explanation.

'That wouldn't be the sheriff from town, would it? He didn't act much to me like he enjoyed havin' us around.'

The cry was not repeated.

Alan eased ahead, but slowly now and with caution. Not until he heard the gunshot did he stop again, and then only for a moment as he and John Bristow drew their handguns and waited until they detected the sound of a running horse coming in their direction.

Bristow said, 'Alf!' and swung to the ground with his carbine. As he dropped to one knee he muttered to himself. 'Comstock, you son of a bitch, big as you are, even in this poor light I can nail you.'

He cocked the carbine and waited, as did Gardea and Bowman.

Alf went past in a run sitting twisted in the saddle with his sixgun poised as he sought a sighting of his pursuers. He had expected something like this so he wasn't as rattled as he might otherwise have been.

He disappeared in the settling night heading straight for the ranch yard. For a long interval no other riders appeared, and when they did Alan swung off, yanked Bowman to the ground and shoved him toward John Bristow. The rangeboss looked up in quick anger. Alan said, 'Too many, John.'

He was correct. There were at least nine horsemen in pursuit of Alf Olmstead; they went past in a blurry shadow of drumming hooves. At least nine of them.

Bristow's carbine barrel tipped toward the ground as he slowly arose looking after the band of horsemen. 'What in hell,' he said very slowly.

Alan turned, stepped into the stirrup and settled across leather. He led his companions back the way they had come in an easy lope. Once, far ahead, they heard another gunshot. It was now too dark for accurate shooting, but that had to be pure speculation. What intrigued Alan Gardea was that whoever had fired those shots had drawn no return fire. This was as encouraging as it was baffling.

He turned once as they were following the band of hard-riders up ahead, caught a wink of weak starlight off metal and called to John that they had riders behind them.

Bristow twisted from the waist, saw nothing and settled forward. Whoever might be back there was a hell of a distance back. It was something to be concerned about but not especially worried about.

They had the yard in sight before they heard horsemen milling in front of the barn. Lights came to life among the *jacals* but not at the main house, whose three-feet thick adobe walls blocked all but the loudest sounds. And there were no lights in the barn area as Alan led his companions toward the yard without dropping back from his lope.

Someone swore defiantly from inside the dark barn and accompanied that with a warning in English. 'You come toward this barn and we'll blow your heads off!'

Alan, John Bristow and their reluctant companion approached the barn, were seen by the band of men temporarily stopped in their tracks by the men inside the barn, and one man moved away from the tie-rack as he recognized Gardea.

'It's Burt Evans, Alan. Comstock come to the jailhouse an' told me Charley Schilling was riding toward town ... We saw him; he rode into the yard ahead of us ... Alan, I got to take him back with me.'

John Bristow swung to the ground, up-ended his Winchester and slid it into the saddle-boot, stepped to the head of his horse and wagged his head at the sheriff. 'That son of bitch got you to do his manhunt for him. Where is he?'

Bowman made a sweeping gesture with one arm. 'Back out there somewhere.'

Gardea and the sheriff ignored these remarks as they faced one another. Alan said, 'You want the man you chased down here?' He did not wait for a reply but looked toward the barn and called. 'Alf.'

Olmstead appeared out of the darkness. Sheriff Evans, like most of his possemen, knew Olmstead. The closer he got to them the more they stared.

Alan said, 'Burt, there's the man you chased. Are you goin' to tell me one of my riders can't ride to town?'

The sheriff looked Olmstead over from head to heels. One of his possemen from Nowhere said, 'That's Alf Olmstead, for Chris'sake, Burt.'

The sheriff's face reddened, which was not noticeable. He faced Gardea again, and jerked his head. The pair of them walked out to the middle of the yard before Sheriff Evans whirled and spoke.

'Alan, you got Schilling out here somewhere. It's only a matter of time before I'm notified by the governor down in Santa Fé that I got to find Schilling an' turn him over to Comstock. I don't know what this was all about tonight, but partner, you're diggin' an awful deep hole for you'n me to fall into. Where is he?'

Alan hung fire over his reply. A light had come to life over at the main house. 'He doesn't stand a chance, Burt. He's flat on his back shot up bad. Ask Doc Emerson. He'll tell you Charley Schilling will sure as hell bleed to death if he's moved. Especially by someone like that deputy from Wyoming.'

Sheriff Evans also turned to watch the light at the main house. When he turned back he shook his head. 'I can't let an order for extradition just set on my desk. All right, I'll talk to Doc, but Alan, the next time I come out here, bad-off or not I'll have to haul Schilling back with me.'

They returned to the area of the barn where none of the riders from town had seemed to have moved, and they probably hadn't; not with the knowledge that only the Good Lord knew how many men with weapons were watching from the barn's interior darkness.

One man started forward as though to approach Sheriff Evans, and John Bristow's arm shot out in an arm grip to stop him. Bristow hissed a warning. 'Not a damned sound or I'll crack your skull!'

Willard Bowman stood helplessly as the men from Nowhere mounted and straggled eastward through the night on their way back the way they had come. Disgruntled, disgusted and sullen.

Alf Olmstead was leaning on the tie-pole when Alan and his rangeboss met there. He blew out a ragged sigh and said, 'Good thing it was dark. One of 'em tried to wing me.'

From behind them *vaqueros* appeared in the front barn opening, Juan Aguilar out front with a Winchester in the crook of his arm. They said nothing. Alan turned; they deserved to know whatever they had not already pieced together, so he told them the entire story.

That hard-eyed man who had offered to scout up Escalante Canyon at the marking ground, spoke quietly. 'Good thing they didn't try stormin' the barn, Alan.'

Another man, dark as old leather and with a heavy accent spoke in a cross between the two languages of the South-west. '*Mira, jefe*, I didn't know what to do when I saw it was the sheriff.'

Another *vaquero* said in Spanish, 'Thank God you did nothing.'

John Bristow told them all to go back to bed, and as they walked away he spoke to Alan Gardea. 'The damned noose is closing, Alan. Unless we want to fight the law an' maybe after that the whole damned army ... Tell you what I think: they know he's here, an' Comstock proved tonight he's as *coyote* as they come. Schilling's got to be hid out somewhere else. Sooner or later the sheriff's goin' to ride into the yard with Comstock an' a search warrant.'

Alan nodded. The idea of moving Charley Schilling had occurred to him, and he believed the serving of a search warrant to be imminent.

He told the rangeboss good-night and crossed toward the main house.

There were now several lamps alight over there, and Maria was standing in the doorway like a dark avenging angel as Alan entered the patio. She said not a word as she stepped aside for him to enter the lighted *sala* where his mother was sitting very erect in an old chair that was black with age and polishing, whose arms and back had been painstakingly carved by some long-gone artisan.

Alan tossed his hat aside, sat down and smiled at the two women. Neither of them smiled back. He made a gesture as he explained what had happened, and Maria sprang on that at once.

'You could have gotten Olmstead killed. Then what, *niño*?'

Alan was tired, frustrated and, of less immediate concern, very hungry. He scowled at the burly *mestizo* woman. 'It did not happen.'

Maria was ready to speak again when Dorotea Gardea addressed her son. 'What happens now?'

Alan shrugged. 'Maybe an extradition order from Santa Fé. Maybe another visit from the sheriff with a search warrant.'

Dorotea's response to those remarks startled both her son and Maria Escobar. 'Then we move him. I've been wanting to visit the Dougherties for a long time. My brothers and cousins and my mother, who's very old now.'

Maria was clearly aghast; Dorotea's son eyed his mother with mixed emotions. That would resolve the issue of hiding Charley Schilling; it also revealed his mother's concern about trouble coming to Charley Schilling. She had answered too swiftly, had come to the rescue of their guest too quickly.

Alan's surprise was not as deep nor understanding as Maria's was. She started to protest. '*Señora*, you can't go outside the law. Alan's already brought enough …'

'In the dark,' Dorotea said, cutting across Maria's protest. 'We will get the coach ready. Blankets and quilts for him to lie on … Maria, I'd like to have you with me.'

The dark woman regarded her mistress solemnly and barely inclined her head.

8 Riders

They accomplished it without awakening the *vaqueros*. Alan harnessed the team and hitched them to the coach. He threw hay in the back and placed a tarp atop it, then drove the rig over to the gateless opening in the patio wall.

Dorotea and Maria, bundled against the cold, helped carry Charley Schilling to the coach and get him gently placed atop the straw. He rolled his eyes at Alan but said nothing. There was nothing to say. Charley had already protested when Alan's mother had awakened him. He had protested her involvement but he might as well have spoken to a stone wall.

As Alan stood in the late-night chill watching his mother and Maria Escobar leave the yard, a very large, dark shadow materialized behind him. Juan Aguilar, a light sleeper, had heard noises, had gotten dressed and armed to investigate.

He had watched everything from the shadows and as the wagon headed northeast he spoke quietly behind Alan Gardea. 'They should not go alone, *jefe*.'

Alan turned, saw the large man and nodded his head. Without anything more passing between them the large *vaquero* walked briskly toward the barn and Alan struck out for the empty house.

With Sheriff Evans and the Wyoming riders returning to town he anticipated no trouble for his mother. Her route would bypass Nowhere on an angling north-easterly route. He was nevertheless thankful Juan Aguilar would be outriding for them.

He got something to eat then went to bed. The day had been hard enough to get through, but having it carry on over into the night would have worn out a horse.

He slept until past sunrise, something he rarely did, and by the time he'd eaten and was walking toward the barn where his riders were already saddling, he felt revived. The lingering autumn chill may have had something to do with that.

John Bristow met him at the tie-rack wearing a quizzical expression. Without a word John pointed to the tracks of steel tyres. Alan told him what they had done late last night and John bobbed his head. That would account for the absence of Juan Aguilar. He turned as a rider led two horses from the barn and handed Bristow the reins to one of them.

'We'll be at the marking ground,' he told Alan as he swung across his horse. 'We can quit early – just in case.'

As the riders left the yard Alan knew the comments would fly thick and fast when they were no longer in his hearing.

It was the first time in ages since he had felt alone, and in fact he wasn't; the *mestizo* women and that old retired *vaquero* from his father's era were going about their chores.

He returned to the house, made fresh coffee and took a cup out to the patio with him. The sun was climbing, the chill was being overcome by pleasant new-day warmth, and the old *vaquero* came to the gateless opening, saw Alan sitting there and spoke in Spanish. 'Riders from the east, *Señor*. Not many, maybe four or five.'

Alan put the cup aside. 'Get your rifle and hide in the barn,' he told the old man, and left the patio without an additional explanation. But none was required, the old man had been most of his life on the Gardea ranch. Alan's father had acted, and spoken, the same way a number of times. It meant trouble and the old man hastened to his *jacal* to take down the long-barrelled old rifle from pegs above his bed, without speaking to the other old man there, who saw him go briskly to the barn.

When the riders entered the yard Alan was leaning on the tie-rack. He had recognized Deputy Comstock before they got close, and eased off the tie-down on his sixgun as he waited.

The large, bearded man stopped, placed both hands atop the saddlehorn and regarded Gardea over an interval of bleak silence before he said, 'We come ahead of the sheriff.' Comstock's face showed sardonic toughness. 'Just in case him an' you pee through the same knothole. We been told in town Messicans stick together. Maybe the sheriff, knowin' everybody, might play favourites.'

Alan was gazing dispassionately at the big man on the big horse when his attention was diverted by the far-out movement of a solitary rider approaching at a loose gallop.

He said, 'He's behind you out a ways.' As the riders twisted to look out there, Alan also said, 'It's the sheriff.'

Behind him there was a rustle of faint sound from the shadows in the barn. Alan turned, then faced forward as Deputy Comstock said, 'We're goin' to paw over this place from top to bottom. He's bringin' a search warrant.' As he said this Comstock's little eyes puckered in cold amusement. 'Even down here lawmen got to abide by the law. I told him last night I'd sign the warrant an' he'd have to serve it.'

Before Alan could speak, if he'd intended to, the big man also said, 'An' after that, I'm goin' to swear out a warrant for that rangeboss of yours. For murder, Mister Gardea.'

Alan stared. 'Who did he murder?'

'That feller who got shot down below where that old man keeps goats.'

Alan's stare widened. 'What are you talking about? That was Schilling fighting for his life. My rangeboss was right here in the yard.'

Comstock chuckled deep in his chest. 'Well, now,

Mister Gardea, these lads with me all saw him down there; saw him shoot my rider. That's four witnesses.'

Alan was still gazing at the bearded large man when Burt Evans loped into the yard, pulled down to a halt and swung off his horse to lead it forward as he said, 'Good-morning, Alan.'

Gardea regarded Sheriff Evans. He nodded without speaking. Burt Evans was uncomfortable, had been since he'd been forced to comply with the law which required him to act on the search warrant the large man from Wyoming had demanded be written for his signature.

Evans said, 'I guess Mister Comstock told you I'd be along.'

Alan still said nothing.

'Well; I got to search the ranch, Alan. If you got that fugitive hid around here, I got to tell you when I find him, I also got to haul you back for being an accessory. That's the law.'

Someone tried to smother a cough deep inside the barn's gloomy interior, and every man sitting outside looked in the direction of that cough, and one rider spoke fretfully to Deputy Comstock. 'I thought you said his riders left the yard.'

Comstock reddened and swung to glare at the speaker, but it was Alan Gardea who said, 'Deputy, you're going to owe your riders double wages for having them spy on me.' He then turned towards Sheriff Evans. 'Go ahead, Burt, the door's open at the main house ... But none of these men do any searching unless you've deputized them. Have you?'

Sheriff Evans shook his head as Comstock leaned to dismount. Alan said, 'Stay on that horse! Our sheriff will make the search. I had most likely ought to tell you, Mister Comstock, in this country when you ride into the yard of someone who doesn't want you there, you can be arrested for trespassing.'

Comstock did not dismount but he snorted his disdain. 'Mister, your trouble is just beginning.'

Alan nodded to Burt Evans. 'Search the place. Just be careful when you go into the barn.' He did not explain that and Burt Evans did not glance into the barn; he loped his reins and struck out for the main house.

The sun was climbing, the front of the barn was not protected from heat by the trees. Comstock and his riders would be uncomfortable before long. Alan would eventually allow them to dismount because a horse's back was not a chair; standing motionless in one place with a lot of weight on its back was harder on a horse than being ridden.

Before Sheriff Evans returned from the main house Comstock said. 'Where'd you hide the carcass of one of my men? Mister, I'm goin' to file a formal complaint against you for murder.'

Alan smiled thinly. 'Who did I murder?'

'Feller named Willard Bowman.'

'When did I do that?'

'Yestiddy afternoon some time. Or last night.'

'And your riders will stand witness to that too, will they?'

Before Comstock could reply Burt Evans returned from the house. He did not say a word as he faced Alan Gardea; he held up a small bloody cloth.

Alan nodded his head. 'That old man named Madrigal who has goats down near where Mister Comstock's men tried to kill Charley Schilling, cut himself.'

Evans said nothing but Comstock made that derisive snort again. 'An' what's his bloody cloth doin'' in your house?'

'My mother is a *curandera*. People come to her from all over to be cared for.'

Comstock turned a scowling face toward Burt Evans. 'What the hell is he talkin' about?'

'A *curandera*,' explained Evans, 'cures people. Looks after the sick, the injured.' He stuffed the little cloth into a pocket and walked away in the direction of the *jacals*.

Comstock and his riders watched him go. Alan finally said, 'Get down. Don't do anything foolish, any of you. Get down and stand in plain sight.'

The men dismounted; several of them eyed the dark interior of the old barn, but the big Wyoming lawman bit off a chew, tongued it into his cheek and watched Sheriff Evans go from *jacal* to *jacal*, where he was met by dark, stocky women whose black eyes mirrored defiance. He spoke to several in Spanish and got no replies.

Comstock clearly did not like the time being spent in this one-man search. He'd had in mind he and his riders conducting the manhunt. The longer he stood in the autumn sun the more uncomfortable he became, and as Sheriff Evans approached one of the last *jacals*, Comstock glared malevolently at Alan Gardea.

'You got him hid. Maybe in the barn loft. Maybe somewhere out a ways. Mister, I'm not leavin' this yard until we have him.'

Alan continued to lean on the tie-rack. He hadn't moved since the riders had entered the yard and he did not move now as he said, 'Remember the first time you rode in here looking for trouble?' Alan jerked his head rearward. 'Go ahead, walk into the barn. Search the loft if you care to.'

One of the Wyoming gunmen gently shook his head. Whether Comstock remembered or not, this man did. That barn had made a deep impression on him the first time he'd been in Gardea's yard, and again last night – and someone sure as hell was in there. He had coughed. Maybe Gardea's entire riding crew was in there. The posseman said, 'Let the sheriff do it, Clem. I ain't goin' in there.'

Comstock turned. His riders looked stonily back. Evidently the complaining man was not alone. Comstock spat amber, did not speak and waited as Burt Evans was returning from his search before he called to him. 'In the barn, Sheriff.'

Evans did not slacken stride nor change direction. When he was out front again he shook his head at the Wyoming lawman. 'He's not here. I found that old goat-herder in the *jacal* of another old man who wasn't there. He told me his *burro* bucked him off in a thornpin thicket.'

Alan listened and gave thanks for the quick-wittedness of old Augustino Madrigal, who had almost certainly heard the talk among the riders and knew who the large bearded man was, along with his gringo possemen. He also knew Sheriff Evans, and when the lawman had appeared at the *jacal* of the old *vaquero* who was in the barn with his rifle, and asked if Madrigal had injured himself, the old man had told a splendid lie and offered to lower his britches to show Sheriff Evans his thornpin punctures.

Burt Evans was content to take the old man's word, and that too Alan Gardea gave silent thanks for.

Comstock glared. 'You went through all them shacks an' the main house an' come up with nothing? Sheriff, give me one hour an' me'n my lads'll flush that damned murderer out. Take my word for it.'

A *mestizo* woman stood out front of a *jacal* with a hand shading her eyes. She called softly to Alan in Spanish. 'Look you, *patrón*, they are many.'

Everyone turned. Even old Augustino Madrigal who had come to stand in the doorway of the other old man's *jacal*, was prompted to do this by the call of the woman.

None of the Wyoming men made a sound. Sheriff Evans squinted from beneath his lowered hatbrim and said, 'You recognize 'em, Alan?'

Gardea replied quietly. 'Pat Dougherty and his riders. If it's the whole crew, there'll be maybe eight or ten of them.'

Deputy Comstock spat out his cud, faced fully around and watched as the distant horsemen hauled down out of a lope to a steady walk. 'Who,' he asked Burt Evans, 'Is Pat Dougherty?'

Alan answered before Sheriff Evans could. 'My mother was a Dougherty. That will be my uncle and his *vaqueros*.'

Comstock watched the bunched-up crowd of horsemen, and swore under his breath as one of his possemen said, 'Clem, it's gettin' awful crowded out here.'

'We'll get what we come for,' growled the large lawman. 'This ain't none of their concern, whoever they are.'

Burt Evans watched the oncoming horsemen for a long while before turning toward Alan Gardea. 'Dougherty's place is a long ride from here.'

Alan nodded. 'Almost thirty miles.'

'They left before sun-up, Alan.'

'We visit back and forth, Burt. You ought to know that by now.'

'Did you know they were coming?'

'No.'

'Why the whole riding crew?'

'Maybe they heard I was having a little trouble, Burt. In a few minutes they'll be in the yard and you can ask them.'

Evans rolled his eyes. He'd encountered this cohesiveness before, and while the local stockmen responded more quickly to trouble one of their neighbours might be having, if there was a blood tie …

Comstock stood wide-legged. Someone coughed inside the barn again. One or two Wyoming riders looked worriedly back but no one else did.

The horsemen entering the yard through tree shade were heavily armed, unsmiling. Two were *gringos*, the remainder were *vaqueros* of dark skin and black eyes.

Sheriff Evans walked ahead to make an interception, but the raw-boned man with the carroty hair with streaks of grey rode past him as though he had not seen Evans, and only drew rein when he was north of the tie-rack a couple of yards, where he looked from face to face and finally nodded at Alan.

'*Qué paso*?' he asked. What's passing, or as *gringos* said, "What's happening?"

Alan smiled. The carroty-haired man was his Uncle Patrick. Alan replied also in Spanish. 'Did my mother see you, *Tio*?'

'*Si*, so early in the morning even the chickens were not up. Who are these *gringos*?'

Alan switched to English. 'This one is a deputy sheriff from Wyoming and these other ones are his …'

'Ah,' the raw-boned older man said, smiling around, and switched back to Spanish. 'Do they understand Spanish?'

'No. I don't think so.'

'Well then, suppose two or three of my riders escort

Sheriff Evans back to town so we can then deal with these outlanders with salt on their backs?'

Sheriff Evans shook his head at the older man astride the *silla vaqueros* with its immense saddlehorn. 'I stay as long as you stay,' he exclaimed in English and Patrick Dougherty smiled warmly.

'You don't want to see this, Burt, my sister told us about the trouble these men have made.'

Burt's eyes widened. 'She's over at your place?'

The affable man with startlingly blue eyes switched back to Spanish. 'Yes. With Juan Aguilar and Maria Escobar. It is a visit long overdue.'

The sheriff got two lines across his forehead.

'Just Maria and Juan Aguilar?' he asked, and got an even broader smile, more conspiratorial now.

'No, with an injured man, friend. Listen to me, *compañero*, go back. I don't like what I see here and I know of only one way to cure it. Please now, old friend, just ride back to town.'

Deputy Comstock's eyes blazed. 'Gawddamit, talk English. You there, Dougherty. You got no business here. This is the work of the law. We don't need no help an' we don't want no interference.'

For a long time Alan's uncle sat leaning on his saddlehorn regarding the big bearded man, then he slowly dismounted, handed his reins to a *vaquero* and walked slowly and deliberately up to Clement Comstock. He was smiling.

Burt Evans started forward. Alan caught his arm and pulled him back.

Comstock reached slowly to brush back his coat on the right side. The man with the carroty hair made no move toward his holstered Colt, but when his arm came up there was a ten-inch knife in it, sharpened on both sides. Its handle was a deer's foot, with the hair on and two small cloven hooves at the top of the handle.

Comstock sneered. 'Greaser toothpick?' he asked.

Dougherty's smile faded a little at a time. 'I'll speak English. You son of a bitch go for that gun or get on your horse and get out of this yard.'

One of the other Wyoming men let his breath out in a hiss. Comstock was fast and deadly with his sixgun, but the man with grey-streaked reddish hair was holding that wicked blade less than a foot from Comstock's soft parts.

Maybe the fast draw could beat the knife and maybe it couldn't, but one thing was a gut-cinch, even if Comstock managed to clear leather with his sixgun, all the other man had to do was lean slightly and push.

Whether the big deputy from Wyoming could get off a shot, this time it wasn't going to matter who was fastest, only who would be left, and the yard was full of unsmiling armed men.

9 A Night Visitor

No one moved or seemed to be breathing as Sheriff Evans quietly said, 'Comstock, be very careful. The odds against you are ten to one.'

That Wyoming posse-rider who had sighed also spoke to the big bearded man. 'Clem, leave it be.'

The large man stood defiantly facing Patrick Dougherty when he scornfully said, 'You'd side with a bunch of Messicans?'

Patrick Dougherty relaxed slightly without moving the knife. 'Get on your horse. Get out of this yard. Unless you're tired of living.'

Comstock remained rooted for what seemed to be an extremely long time, then abruptly turned his back on Dougherty and swung into the saddle. From up there he said, 'Mister, this mealy-mouthed sheriff of yours ain't fit to wear a badge.' As he gathered his reins he added a little more. 'Let's see how you make out against the army.'

As he led his possemen out of the yard in a lope, those left behind watched him go. Dougherty sheathed his knife and shook his head at his nephew. Sheriff Evans had a question for the man with the grey-streaked carroty hair. 'You got Schilling at your ranch?'

Dougherty eyed the lawman in silence.

'Because if you have,' Burt Evans said, 'It'll make you part of a conspiracy to break the law.'

Dougherty finally spoke. 'Burt, it's not breakin' the law that worries me, it's that oversized son of a bitch coming down here like he's God Almighty.'

Evans did not relent. 'If you hand Schilling over … Patrick, I got a warrant for him, and that big horse's rear wasn't just shooting off his mouth. I've straddled the fence until I got saddle-sores, but I'm not going up against the army.'

Dougherty smiled. 'You won't have to.'

'Won't I?'

'No. The nearest army post is at Fort Union, sixty miles from Nowhere.'

'I see. And when they get here Schilling won't be around.'

'Something like that,' replied Dougherty, and faced his nephew. 'Your mother would like you to come back with us.'

Alan shook his head. 'No. This is where Comstock will make trouble. It's not just me, it's my people.'

Dougherty went to his horse, straddled it and gazed at his nephew. 'You'll be on your own, Alan. It's a long ride for us both ways. Let me leave some men here.'

'I have a riding crew, but I'm grateful for the offer.'

Dougherty threw a hard look at Burt Evans. 'We'll ride part way back to town with you.'

Evans mounted and shook his head at Alan Gardea, then rode out of the yard with the Dougherty *vaqueros*.

The old *vaquero* came out of the barn and leaned on the tie-rack with his rifle. In Spanish he said, 'That came very close, *Patrón*.'

Alan smiled. 'Bring your houseguest to the patio. We'll share some wine.'

The old man hobbled off as solemn as an owl and Alan returned to the main house, hungry again. He had time enough to eat, wash and shave before a timid knock sounded on the massive old oaken door. He took a decanter and three glasses to the patio.

As he filled the glasses and handed them around he spoke to Augustino Madrigal in Spanish. 'Look you, how did you tell the lawman that little bloody rag was yours?'

Madrigal grinned self-consciously. 'I lied, *Patrón*. From the door of my host's house I saw him show you the rag. Later when I knew he was among the houses I made up the lie and he believed it.' The old man shrugged. 'At least he did not want me to lower my trousers to show him the scratches.'

Both the old men laughed and Alan smiled, refilled their glasses and handed each of them a gold coin. No false inhibition prevented either of them from accepting the money, and as they left the patio heading for their *jacal* they compared the coins, bit them to be sure they weren't counterfeit – which perhaps as much as half the money was – and discussed the pleasure of sharing a bottle of *pulque* the old *vaquero* had hidden away. Not because it was precious to him, but because during his youth when Alan Gardea's father had ruled, liquor of any kind except wine was forbidden, and the old *vaquero* like most old men, had only lately been able to rid himself of the rules he had obeyed most of his life.

When John Bristow returned with the riders from the marking ground, they heard from half-a-dozen people what had transpired in the yard during their absence.

John cleaned up, ate supper and with daylight fading approached the main house. When Alan met him the rangeboss looked stern. 'We should have stayed here,' he said. 'Suppose your mother's kinsmen had not arrived?'

Alan smiled. 'You sound like Maria Escobar.'

Bristow was not placated. 'Alan, maybe Comstock will send for the army. My guess is that he'll try to get even with you, and we already know how he fights – in the dark or from ambush.'

Alan changed the subject. 'Where's Bowman?'

'Chained to the *jacal* we put him in last night.'

Alan offered wine which his rangeboss declined. Alan got some for himself before continuing their discussion. 'John, the army's not going to find anything. The Dougherties will know when soldiers arrive.'

'Alan,' responded the rangeboss, sounding almost like a parent scolding a wayward child, 'I understand what you folks are doing for Charley Schilling, and I, for a damned fact, appreciate it. But what started out as a decent gesture is turning into something a hell of a lot more serious. It's not just the disagreeable deputy from Wyoming – hell, I can sock him away – it's everyone else; your mother, your mother's kinsmen, our people here on the ranch ...'

Alan drained his glass and turned it slowly in his hand as though studying it. Bristow had left something out; the possibility of a direct order to Burt Evans from Santa Fé to find Schilling, which Alan knew he could do, and turn him over to the men from Wyoming. Before he could speak John Bristow said, 'Bein' stubborn ain't an answer to anything. Let me go get Schilling and haul him down over the line. Even the army can't touch him then.'

Except for one thing the rangeboss's suggestion was sound enough. 'You'd never get a mile from the Dougherty place, John. Comstock'll figure it out and have someone watching the yard over yonder the way he's been watching us.'

Bristow threw up his hands. 'That leaves just one thing. I'll sock Comstock away.'

Alan gazed at his foreman. 'He doesn't get ten yards from his possemen.'

Bristow shrugged. 'I'll take Juan with me.'

'It won't be just Comstock, John.'

'All right. I'll take Alf Olmstead. He's got reason to want to repay them for shootin' at him.'

Alan walked his rangeboss to the yard as he said, 'Let me do a little figuring, John. I'll see you in the morning.'

Bristow did not walk away, he stood a moment regarding his employer and sounded disgusted as he said, 'In the morning.'

Alan left the yard at dusk, covered the entire distance to Nowhere without incident, sought Sheriff Evans and told him he wanted to swear out a warrant for Deputy Comstock.

Burt looked troubled. 'On what grounds? Hell, this damned mess is gettin' worse by the hour.'

'For attempted murder.' At the way the sheriff's eyebrows shot up, Alan said, 'He tried to kill Alf Olmstead.'

Sheriff Evans sat down at his desk. 'For Chris'sake, Alan.'

'How about trespassing?'

Evans shook his head. 'You don't know he tried to shoot Olmstead. As for trespassing, it's done every day by all of us; nobody knows exactly where property boundaries are, and if they did it wouldn't matter. Fools go where they have to go. Not just down here but everywhere else. It's been goin' on for a hundred years and will continue to go on for another hundred years ... What are you trying to do?'

'Get Comstock locked up.'

'Why? You got to come up with something better'n you've ...'

'Because there are men who are going to kill him, Burt. Sooner or later someone will kill him. The longer he's down here the more enemies he makes.'

Sheriff Evans rolled his eyes upwards before speaking again. 'Do you know for a fact someone's out to shoot him?'

Alan side-stepped a direct answer. 'You know as well as I do all he's done since coming down here is get everyone's temper up.'

Sheriff Evans sat a moment staring at his hands atop the desk. Eventually he said, 'To make a charge like attempted murder hold up you got to have witnesses.'

'I'll get them,' Gardea replied, and again the lawman looked prayerfully upwards. 'The same way he got witnesses to the charge that my rangeboss shot that man of his down by the old man's goat ranch.'

Sheriff Evans arose, face reddening, went to the gun-rack on the wall and turned back. 'Alan, I've tried helping you in this mess.'

'I know it and appreciate it, Burt.'

'But gawddamit you're making it worse. I don't personally care a damn about Charley Schilling. It's Comstock and what he can do that worries me. If he gets the army up here there'll be hell to pay. Even if he don't, an' I get a direct order from the governor to hand Schilling over to Comstock, I'll be holding a losing hand. I don't want to go out there and buck your mother's tribe. Any way I turn, Alan, I'm goin' to end up with my teat in a wringer.'

The sheriff returned to his chair and leaned on the desk looking at his visitor. 'Maybe right from the start I should have done different; made up a big posse and gone out to your place, found Schilling and brought him back.'

'The trip at that time would have killed him, Burt.'

'I already told you, I don't give a damn about Charley Schilling.'

Alan shoved up out of his chair. 'Are you going to work up that murder warrant against Comstock, or not?'

Evans gazed at his old friend a long time before slowly shaking his head. 'If every rider you got swears they saw Comstock shoot at Alf Olmstead, it won't be enough. You'd have to get the possemen who rode with me that night to take the same oath, an' they wouldn't do it. It was dark, Alan, no one knows who shot at Alf Olmstead.'

Alan went to the jailhouse door, opened it as he turned and said, 'They're going to kill him, Burt. If he was locked up for a week or two, it'd be easier on you and easier on me.'

Sheriff Evans did not need a warrant to arrest Deputy Comstock. If someone swore one out and signed it, he would make the apprehension, but if he arrested Comstock for some breach of local law all he'd need would be a few men to offset Comstock's possemen, and one of the sawed-off shotguns on the north wall of his office.

He went up to the saloon, got a bottle and took to a table in a gloomy part of the saloon. He was not much of a drinking man, and he did not drink much now. He worried instead.

If Alan Gardea was right; if someone shot and killed the Wyoming lawman, there would be more trouble around Nowhere and its countryside than a person could shake a stick at, not because Comstock had been killed, but because the local sheriff hadn't prevented it. Sure as death and taxes, people would learn that he had been warned Comstock might be killed. Things like that had a way of circulating no matter how tight-mouthed the principals might be.

It was a pleasant night. The usual hint of autumn cold was lacking, every star was hooked into place overhead and coyotes, which had long since abandoned seeking birthing grounds because calves were dropped in February, had to travel farther for carrion, or mice, or rabbits, or, in a pinch, snakes and fallen baby birds.

The moon lacked a quarter of being full but starshine made up the difference as Alan loped homeward over a countryside bathed in soft, pewter light. He was perhaps a hundred yards from the great standing old unkempt trees when he heard the gunshot.

Instinct told horsemen they were perfect targets. Alan swung off and waited a moment for another shot. When there was none he led his horse forward. He was careful, utilized every tree-shadow and got to the barn without incident.

A candle wavered to light in one of the *jacals*. Moments later other weak light appeared elsewhere around the compound.

After caring for the horse Alan remained in the barn. If there was danger anyone attempting to cross the yard would be a perfect target.

The night was still and soundless. Several additional lights wavered to brightness among the *jacals*. The main house was dark. There were serving women over there but either through prudence, or the proven inability to hear much through the massively thick walls, no light showed.

A wavery figure appeared behind the barn, moonlighted only as a moving silhouette. Alan moved close and when the shadow came closer he fisted his sidearm and cocked it. The sound of a gun being cocked, once heard, was never forgotten.

Someone breathed a quick prayer. The moving shadow became very still. Alan asked in Spanish who was there. The reply came in a gush of relief. 'Augustino Madrigal. Is that you, *Patrón*?'

Alan eased the dog of his Colt down, leathered the weapon and moved toward the rear barn opening as he said, 'What in hell are you doing out here?'

The old man had no difficulty distinguishing the sound of irritation in the question, answered in a wavery voice. 'I went outside to pee. There was someone sneaking around over by the wagon shed. I watched and waited. He came around the shed and disappeared inside. While he was unable to see me, I hurried past the barn to the back of the shed.'

'Were you armed, *viejo*?'

'*Si*. I borrowed the weapon of my host, who could sleep through the end of the world ... *Patrón*, I was sneaking around to the front of the wagon shed when he must have heard me, or maybe he even saw me. He fired. I heard the bullet strike wood very close and ran back behind the shed ... I never saw him again. I was trying to sneak back to the *jacal* when you caught me.'

Alan sighed. 'Come inside.'

The old man shuffled into the barn. Their eyes were adequately adjusted to the gloom. The old goat-man had an ancient revolver shoved into his waistband. If he hadn't been as dark as he was and if the light had been better Alan would have seen the underlying pallor and the shaking hands.

He told the old man to remain in the barn and went out the back way, along the barn to the rear of the open-fronted wagon shed and waited. There was a sound but it came from a considerable distance out, northward. It had to be a running man; animals did not wear spurs. He started toward the sound but with little hope of success. The fleeing man certainly had a horse out there somewhere.

He did have, but before reaching it he heard Alan in pursuit and stopped, turned and waited, gun up and steady. When he fired the slug was a yard wide of the sound. Alan fired at the muzzle blast twice. The first bullet was close enough to make the unseen target spring up with a curse. The second shot, following the sound of the swearing, brought a clearly audible gasp.

Alan changed direction and slowed his approach to minimize sounds.

The night visitor was sitting on the ground with a large rock at his back. His gun was on the ground as he tried to stop the bleeding of a wounded upper leg.

Alan approached until he could see his target. The wounded man did not look up until Alan said, 'Use your belt. Cinch it as tight as you can.'

In moments the gunman and his captor became, not friends, but allies. Alan knelt, kicked the man's gun away and helped him pull the belt tight enough to stop the bleeding. As he arose, wiping both hands down the outside of his trousers, he looked closely at the night visitor. It was the same posse-rider who warned Deputy Comstock in his yard to let it go; he was the man who had been fearfully holding his breath in the showdown between the Dougherty riders and Deputy Comstock.

The man was in obvious pain. Sweat popped out on his forehead as he stared at Alan Gardea. Without a word Alan hoisted the man to his feet and when he would have crumpled Alan told the man to put an arm across Alan's shoulder as he gripped the night visitor around the waist and started back toward the yard.

There were people waiting. In the forefront were the two old men: the retired *vaquero* and Augustino Madrigal.

Mestizo women wrapped in heavy *rebozos*, watched stoically as Alan leaned his prisoner upon the tie-rack.

John Bristow, in boots and pants, jammed his Colt back into its holster and told some of the women to take the injured man to his *jacal* and care for his injury.

As they moved to obey, others came to help and John faced his employer. 'Do you know who he is?'

'Not his name, only his face.'

John smiled thinly. 'If this keeps up Comstock's goin' to be a mighty lonesome man. Now we got two of his friends. I'll go talk to the son of a bitch. He's got a name and he's got some explainin' to do.'

Alan nodded. He was sticky from the wounded man's blood, and half carrying him from out where the shooting had occurred had left him breathing hard.

10 An Eye for an Eye

The wounded man's name was Jess Coon. He was drowsy from shock and loss of blood, otherwise he might not have answered truthfully. He saw John Bristow take a cup from a woman and approach his cot with it. Jess Coon was thirsty but what John poured down his throat was some kind of Mex liquor that burned like fire as it went down, and almost immediately induced a drowsy well-being.

The bleeding had been stopped by the *mestizo* women. His injury had been bandaged properly and with the chill of dawn approaching someone had lighted a fire in the corner cooking area. Bristow flung an old army blanket over him and accepted a cup of hot coffee from one of the impassive silent women as he sat next to the cot on a little three-legged stool.

'How long was you out there?' Bristow asked, and, as before, got a straightforward reply.

'Since sundown.'

'Why?'

'To kill Gardea.'

The onlookers held their stoic expressions but their eyes went to one another as Bristow sipped coffee before speaking in Spanish to one of the *vaqueros*. 'Bring the other one over here.'

As the *vaquero* departed Jess Coon said, 'Don't nobody in this damned country use English?'

John nodded. 'They all do. But Spanish has been the language down here a hunnert years. Sometimes it's easier. Comstock sent you?'

'Yes. He wants Gardea's hide to hang on the wall.'

'Has he sent someone for the army?'

'I don't know. He don't always tell us what he's figuring. But he was mad enough on the ride back to town to do it.'

When Willard Bowman entered the *jacal* and Jess Coon saw him, his eyes widened. Neither man said a word until the wounded man spoke more strongly than he had heretofore. 'You sold out to them, for Chris'sake? Clem'll drag you half-way back to Wyoming behind his horse.'

Before Bowman could reply Bristow said, 'He didn't sell out. We caught him.'

'Comstock thinks you killed him an' more'n likely hid the carcass.'

'He don't look dead to me,' Bristow replied drily.

Bowman approached the cot, eyed the bandaged leg and wagged his head at the wounded man. 'Clem's been under-estimatin' these folks ever since we got down here. How bad off are you, Jess?'

Bristow answered first. 'He won't set a horse for a month or so.' He arose, drained his cup and put it aside as he regarded the pair of posse-riders. 'Comstock's whittled down to himself and two others.'

The man on his back on the little bed looked up.

'You think that'll scare him off? Let me tell you something, mister: there's a lot of money ridin' on Schilling, an' Clem never quit a manhunt yet.'

John Bristow said drily, 'Three men against half the countryside? We'll bury him, cowboy.'

Coon and Bowman exchanged a glance before Bristow spoke. 'You two are out of it. Count that as a blessing.'

He walked out of the *jacal* followed by most of the riders and the *mestizo* women. One *vaquero* turned in the doorway and jerked his head. Willard Bowman obeyed the unspoken summons. The last thing he said to the wounded man was: 'On the ride down here you was complainin' about ridin' your butt sore. Partner, from here on all you got to do is eat an' sleep. I been here longer'n you. Don't be in any hurry to get back to Clem.'

Jess Coon gazed at the doorway after Bowman had departed, until one of the impassive women brought him some hot broth with a light lacing of *pulque* in it.

John met Alan Gardea at the barn where the riders were bringing in horses. Alan asked about the wounded man. John told him everything he had learned, then leaned on the tie-rack shaking his head. 'If we don't get this over with soon, Alan, them cattle is goin' to have drifted back up where they was.'

Alan smiled. 'Go out, drive in the drift then come back.' At the quizzical gaze he got for saying that, Alan added a little more. 'We'll finish this today if we got to run Comstock down to do it.'

Bristow brightened. This had been what he'd been advocating for a week. He called to the men to rig out and left Alan at the tie-rack as he went back to saddle and bridle the mount he'd used today.

His mood was better than it had been for some

time. Like Sheriff Evans, he did not like waiting until the army arrived.

Neither did Alan Gardea, but his concerns had not been as simple as those of his rangeboss.

The men left the yard in a tight bunch, loped to the marking ground and fanned out to bring in the drift. Because they were experienced stockmen, they accomplished this well before noon and gathered at the cold branding fire to dismount and let the horses 'blow' before starting back.

When Bristow told them all that Alan Gardea had said, Alf Olmstead spoke for them all when he said, 'It's about time.'

Bristow could have agreed with that; instead he mounted to lead the way back to the yard.

He did not look for his employer when they got to the barn. He went directly to his *jacal*, nodded to the women who were looking after the wounded man, took down his Winchester from its pegs and was shoving it into the boot when Jess Coon said drily, 'You goin' coyote huntin', rangeboss?'

John answered without facing around. 'No. We're goin' son-of-a-bitch huntin'. You just lie still, do what the women tell you, and with a little luck by the time we return you'n Willard Bowman will be all that's left.'

Jess Coon watched Bristow leave the *jacal* striding in the direction of the barn. He looked at one of the women and said, 'Don't they ever eat or sleep?'

She looked stoically back without answering.

A bronzed *vaquero* poked his head inside the *jacal* and said something to the women, laughed and walked away. He was carrying a booted saddlegun. Coon asked a woman what the man had said and she shrugged without answering.

Not until they could hear riders leaving the yard did one of the women, younger than the others, come over and interpret. 'He said they are going to shoot the ... *cojones* ... off that big man with the beard.'

Coon frowned. He did not have to ask what that Spanish word meant. She had not put it into English but she hadn't had to. Jess Coon had just learned his first word of Spanish, and unfortunately it was not a word that could be used very often, and never in mixed company.

He asked where they kept Willard Bowman, and the same younger woman, whose eyes were like liquid night, answered when it became obvious none of the older women were going to.

'He is in the house of an old *vaquero*. There are two old men over there. They have him chained to the wall. He is all right.'

'How did they catch him?' Coon asked, and got a soft shrug of handsome shoulders. The pretty woman did not know, or, if she did, she was disinclined to keep their conversation going because the older women were staring at her with disapproval.

The midday autumn warmth was pleasant. From now on only rarely would there be hot days. For loping riders it was perfect weather; their horses did not raise a sweat until they had Nowhere in sight and Alan drew down to a steady walk.

John Bristow came up beside him. 'If they're stayin' at the rooming house, we'd do better to split up. All of us ridin' up out front ... They'll see us sure as hell.'

Alan looked at the older man. He did not ask why his rangeboss had made this suggestion, but clearly John Bristow was no stranger to this kind of trouble.

John took a couple of the men to the livery barn. Alan and Alf Olmstead reached town farther north, up near the west side of the rooming house.

If anyone noticed all the Gardea riders arriving in town no one seemed to be curious about it. That was John Bristow's strategy; any time a heavily armed band of men entered a town in a group, people ducked into buildings or scattered like chickens. The raffish liveryman took Bristow's horse and the animal of his companion, and led them down through his runway to be corralled out back. He happened to look northward where two riders were riding at a dead walk, and recognized one of them – Alan Gardea.

He put the horses in a corral and did not return to his barn but went hurrying up the back alley as far as the jailhouse. He had to beat on the rear door, which was always kept locked, for half a minute before Sheriff Evans opened it, scowling.

Patrick Leary spoke swiftly. 'Gardea's in town with his riders. Two are down at my place, Gardea an' another feller was comin' in on the west side of the hotel.'

Evans nodded, closed and re-locked the door and went directly to the wall rack of weapons on his office wall, took down a shotgun, broke it, shoved in two shells, slammed it closed and dropped a handful of shells into his pocket.

He did not appear in the front roadway with the scattergun. He leaned it just inside the office doorway and closed the door.

Across the road people were milling; on his side of the roadway there were more people, mostly women with knitted shopping bags on their arms. Down at the smithy someone was warping steel over an anvil. The sound was musical and travelled the full length of town.

There were four saddle animals drowsing at the

saloon hitch-rack, and opposite the saloon a pair of old men were sitting in overhang shade outside the harness works, contentedly enjoying their cuds of Kentucky twist.

South of town the midday stagecoach was approaching at a dead walk with the tugs sagging. It was late as usual, but in *mañana*-land this was a matter of slight concern.

Sheriff Evans looked for, and did not see, Alan Gardea or any of his riders, all of whom he knew by sight.

The liveryman would not have been mistaken. He knew the Gardea *vaqueros* as well as the sheriff did.

Under normal conditions Burt Evans would not have been troubled. Gardea and his riders visited town often – but they used the roadways to get there.

Comstock and his riders had rooms at the rooming house. Sheriff Evans sighed and started walking in that direction. There would be no trouble, if that was what Gardea had come to town for, but while the sheriff knew this he was confident Alan Gardea did not know it.

The rooming house proprietor was a widow-woman named Mary Starkey. She had bought the place with the money she had received when her husband had been killed in a train wreck fifteen years before. She had never liked railroad companies and still didn't. She was a large, robust woman, grey and narrow-eyed who viewed all mankind as rutting animals.

When Sheriff Evans appeared in her parlour she eyed him warily. They had always gotten along well enough. In fact she rather liked Burt Evans, who was young enough to be her son. Maybe it was not so much like as it was respect. He had intervened a number of times when her guests had been troublesome. When she saw him in her parlour she nodded, which was as close as she came to smiling. He asked if Alan Gardea had been by. She shook her head.

'He will be,' the sheriff said. 'I'll sit down and wait if you don't mind.'

She didn't mind. 'I'll fetch you a cup of fresh-brewed coffee. Why would he be coming here?'

The sheriff smiled and said he would appreciate the cup of coffee, and after a moment of looking at each other the woman left the parlour.

The wait was longer than Sheriff Evans had expected, because, although he did not know it at the time, the Gardea riders from the lower end of town used the back alley to reach the northern end where the rooming house was, and they did not enter, but lingered outside until they saw Alan enter, leaving Alf Olmstead on the porch.

Burt Evans nodded curtly at Alan, who was finishing his coffee and did not arise nor offer his hand as he said, 'Did you draw up that warrant for Comstock?'

Burt sat down shaking his head. 'I told you it wouldn't work, Alan. Sayin' Comstock shot at your rider an' provin' it are two different things. I know, I know, you could have your riders swear they saw Comstock do it, but they didn't and neither did any of the rest of us ... By the way, if you came to town to find Comstock, you made a long ride for nothing. He left town early this morning.'

Gardea's brows climbed. 'You mean he's quitting?'

'I don't know. All I know is that I saw him leave town with two riders about breakfast time.'

'Up the north road?'

'Yes ... There's still another one around somewhere. Comstock swears you killed him, which I don't believe.'

Alan smiled. 'I've got them both at the ranch. The one Comstock sent out there last night to shoot me, got winged in the leg. He's being taken care of. The other one, Willard Bowman, is living better'n he's lived in a long time. You can have them both any time you want to come out with a wagon and haul them back ... Comstock went up the north road?'

'That's what I said,' the lawman replied, then quickly added more. 'If you're thinkin' he went out to the Dougherty place ...'

'Where else, Burt? He'd travel the north road until he was clear of town, then swing north-easterly.'

'He'd have to be crazy. Your uncle's got a lot of riders. He knew that after what happened in your yard the last time all of us was out there.'

Alan arose, put on his hat and without another word started for the door. Sheriff Evans caught up with him. 'He's not that crazy, Alan. Hell, there's a lot of other directions he could go in.'

'But the other directions don't have Charley Schilling. Burt, Comstock's got two men left, and he's as wily as an old wolf.'

'He'd never ride into your uncle's yard.'

'You're right about that, but this man knows more ways than ten to skin a cat.'

'I'll ride with you.'

Alan opened the door and stepped out on to the porch where Alf Olmstead was leaning. 'We won't need you, Burt. Not if they went out to the Dougherty place.'

As Alan and his rider left the porch, Evans jerked his head sideways and went down along the far side of the rooming house. Sheriff Evans saw Alan and three other men walk in the direction of the alley. He knew every one of them, and what he'd suspected had brought them to town was confirmed by their armaments. He turned back and struck out for the shed behind the jailhouse where he kept two horses.

11 Ghost Canyon

Alan rode in silence for a mile before leaving the road on an eastward angle. There was a reason; there was always a reason, even for accidents, and as he'd said to Burt Evans, Comstock was as wily as a coyote. He knew how many riders his uncle had. Maybe he thought they'd be at a marking ground. This time of year, before cold weather set in, it was customary to round up and work-through cattle, particularly the big slick calves that had been dropped since the previous marking time in February.

Maybe, too, Comstock meant to lie in hiding until nightfall before attempting to find Charley Schilling and take him away.

In Wyoming Deputy Comstock had been in home territory; he knew all the customs and habits of stockmen, but this far south, and assuming he had picked up considerable information, he probably had not learned that large cow outfits maintained a sentinel throughout the dark hours, something which rarely justified the inconvenience, but which had become ingrained after decades of sneak attacks by Indians.

By the time they were on Dougherty range it was time to scout ahead. If Comstock was truly *coyote*, he would watch both ways, up ahead as well as his back trail.

Bristow volunteered but Alan sent Alf Olmstead, and led off into some spindly thickets of wiry chaparral to wait.

John Bristow tucked a neat cud into his cheek and as he pocketed the plug he said, 'He's crazy if he thinks the Dougherties won't have riders out ... Unless he's already scouted-up the yard and found a place to hide until everyone's gone.'

Alan shrugged. It still would be very unhealthy for Comstock to ride into the empty yard, because among the old *haciendados* there were always people around, mostly women, but a few men too, old or crippled, but still men with weapons.

Bristow sprayed amber, squinted at the position of the sun and moved out a short distance on foot, but there was no sign of Alf Olmstead. When he returned and met Alan's look he shrugged. 'He must have gone closer to the yard. That'd take more time.' Bristow wasn't worried. Olmstead had been in the south country a long time; long enough to be careful.

Alan let time pass as he worried increasingly. Olmstead did not have much cover in the direction he had taken. On the other hand he had repped for the Gardea brand a number of times and knew this part of the range as well as Alan or John Bristow knew it.

He waited, worried, and finally told John he was going to scout ahead. Bristow did not demur; he too had begun to worry.

Alan rode from thicket to thicket all the way to an *arroyo* deep enough to have a wide area at its bottom where a sluggish warm-water creek ran and quite a few trees grew.

Down there he saw horse tracks fresh enough to have earth still crumbling inward over the impressions. He rode ahead, eyes on the ground, certain this was the way Olmstead had gone.

The air was clear but trees and flourishing underbrush limited his visibility to a few yards. Once, where the tracks curved around a big old white oak tree, he started up a covey of mountain quail. Their racket startled his horse.

The tracks went to the creek's soft edge. Olmstead had watered his animal here, but had not crossed to the far side of the sluggish little waterway but had turned back and continued on his original course.

This *arroyo* was called *Cañon Fantasmas*. No one was sure how it had gotten its name, that had been lost generations ago, but the name remained, and its implication was that the canyon was haunted: *fantasmas* were ghosts. It was anyone's guess how it had come by that name, but the story Alan had heard from one of his uncle's *vaqueros* as a boy was that some *arrerios* up out of Mexico with their pack mules had made a camp down there to escape mid-summer heat, and had been caught by Apaches who had got belly-down atop the steep sides and had killed every packer and several of the mules.

Their ghosts still moaned there on full-moon nights, the *vaquero* had said, rolling his eyes for emphasis. Neither he nor any of the other Dougherty *vaqueros* would ride anywhere near *Cañon Fantasmas* after sundown, and some would not go near it even in broad daylight.

The *gringos* had several different versions, but with a name like Canyon of Ghosts it was inevitable that fertile imaginations had, over the years, had a field day.

Alan went up the punky soft earth of the creek for several hundred yards and came upon what was supposed to have been the place the Mexican mule-train had been ambushed. There was no sign that a massacre had taken place there. The grass was green and tall; the slopes on both sides were high and crumbly; the heat was greater in the *arroyo* than it had been above it.

Alan paused to re-affirm his bearings, then resumed tracking. *Cañon Fantasmas*, more properly *Cañon de los Fantasmas*, tended to curve eastward in a very gradual way, as though the prehistoric river which had carved it had been too sluggish to undercut banks and chew away places where it could not flow in a straight line.

It was easy to understand Alf Olmstead's reason for staying in the *arroyo* where he would be invisible to riders above it. Its gradual eastward turn approached within a few hundred yards of the Dougherty ranch yard.

It did not occur to Alan that the tracks Alf had been following, and which he saw from time to time in the trampled tall grass, could have been made by anyone other than the Wyoming manhunters, and in this he was correct.

Where he made a misjudgement was in not watching more ahead than watching the fresh tracks of his *vaquero*.

A long-spending gradual curve eastward with trees and underbrush made tracking difficult for a hundred or so yards before the prehistoric creek bed straightened out.

Ahead was a skimpy clearing with stirrup-high grass and no brush nor trees on the floor of the *arroyo*, but stands of both on either side of it.

The tracks led directly across the little clearing. Alan was half-way across before his horse threw up its head, little ears pointing. By then it was too late. Alan drew rein and looked on both sides of the little clearing where overhead sunlight was reflected off steel. He let his breath out slowly. He had ridden into an ambush like a child.

For ten seconds there was neither movement nor sound. During that period of grace Alan cursed himself for not appreciating that Comstock and his riders had used this same *arroyo* to get close enough to the Dougherty yard to make a sortie after nightfall. He was disgusted; both he and his rider had ridden into the lay-by where the Wyoming manhunters were waiting.

The large bearded man stepped into sight on Alan's left side. He was smiling. 'Well now,' he said in an almost amiable tone of voice, 'this is better'n I could have hoped for. Get down off your horse, Gardea. And shuck that sidearm. *Now*!'

Alan dismounted, stepped to the head of his horse and tossed his sixgun into the grass. Deputy Comstock looked positively delighted. 'Two birds with one stone,' he crowed, and called to someone named Curtis to take Gardea's horse into the trees and fetch along Alan's discarded sixgun.

While the hard-faced, sweating manhunter moved to obey, smiling too, Alan said, 'You'd better reconsider, Mister Comstock. You know how many riders my uncle has.'

Comstock's reply indicated that he'd had the Dougherty yard under surveillance even before he came out here.

'Sure we know,' he replied to Alan Gardea. 'An' we know too that the feller with the red hair and the big knife led his riders out more'n an hour ago heading north where they been makin' a gather.' Comstock gloated. 'So isn't no one goin' to rescue you or your rider.'

For the first time Alan understood what had happened to Alf Olmstead. He too had ridden into the trap, but there was no sign of either Alf or his Gardea horse.

Comstock walked away from tree shade directly into bright sunlight as he approached Alan. He was still looking very pleased with himself when he halted, hooked thumbs in his shellbelt and said, 'How'd you know we was out here?'

'It wasn't hard to figure out, Deputy. You were seen leaving town early up the north stage road.'

'Why up here?' the large man asked.

'Because you figured out where Charley Schilling was.'

'Ahhh. When you said that, Gardea, you told me you knew he was out when we'n that damned measly sheriff made his search at your place.'

Alan nodded.

The big man jerked his head sideways. 'Walk toward them trees where I come out. Ahead of me, an' if think you can cut an' run for it, go right ahead and try.'

Alan did as ordered, making no attempt to break free. He turned his head a little and told Comstock the sound of gunfire would carry to his uncle's yard.

Two manhunters, one from the opposite side of the clearing, one from the near side, came into view with carbines low in both hands.

Comstock herded his latest captive into cool shade and told him to sit down. As Alan looked around he saw the Gardea horse Alf Olmstead had been riding.

He sat down looking up at the large, bearded man. 'Where's my rider?'

'Your damned spy, you mean.'

Alan shrugged. 'Where is he?'

'Tied to a tree back a ways. We couldn't take no chance on him hearin' you comin' and let off a warning yell.'

'He all right?'

'Right now he is. So are you all right. But that might not be much longer.' The big man grunted down into a squatting position. His two manhunters remained upright with carbines aimed at Alan Gardea. Maybe Deputy Comstock was enjoying this, but his poker-faced manhunters did not seem to be.

Back out of sight through the trees a horse shifted his stance and several birds flung skyward in fright.

Comstock had time to kill, along with two prisoners. He asked Alan where the rest of his crew were and Alan told him they hadn't yet reached the canyon. Then he also said, 'But they will. They'll be along.'

For the time being this information did not appear to trouble the Wyoming lawman. 'What'd you do with that feller who was spyin' on your yard last night? Killed him like you done the other feller?'

'Willard Bowman and Jess Coon? They're at my place. Coon got hit in the leg. He won't be much good to you or anyone else for a while. Willard Bowman's eating good, getting plenty of rest, and I think he's beginning to have second thoughts about you.'

Comstock's pleasant expression slowly changed. He looked malevolently at Alan Gardea. 'You're so gawddamned smart, ain't you? Well, mister, this here canyon is as far as you're going.'

Alan repeated what he'd said earlier. 'They'll hear a gunshot in Dougherty's yard.'

Comstock made a death's-head grin. 'But they won't hear a rifle barrel crushing your skull, will they?' He arose and walked toward his remaining possemen.

Alan was angry with himself and fearful for the men he'd left in the sickly underbrush. John Bristow would not worry for long before he led off in a search, which could very easily lead him down into the same canyon following the same tracks, until the possemen heard him coming and ambushed him as they'd done Alan and Alf Olmstead.

One of the Wyoming posse-riders sat down with his back to a tree, Winchester balanced loosely on his lap. He asked if Alan had any smoking tobacco. Alan didn't have and that ended their conversation for a while, until the posseman asked a question. 'Did you think you was bein' smart when you told Clem that Will Bowman was gettin' fed up with him? Mister, a couple words of advice; don't stir Clem Comstock up. I've seen him beat men to death an' he's pure death with a gun.'

Alan said, 'Thanks for the advice. You're going to sit down here until nightfall then try to find Charley Schilling in the Dougherty yard?'

The posseman seemed to think about his answer before he gave it, and his obvious conclusion was that no matter what he said, Gardea would be dead shortly. 'Yeah, somethin' like that. It'll be chancy. That Dougherty feller's got a big crew.'

Alan nodded about the risk. 'There's something else you might want to ponder: if you get Schilling, which I doubt will happen, but if you do, and there's trouble in the yard, my uncle won't wait for a town-posse, he'll ride you fellers down.'

The posse-rider squirmed a little, felt a rock under

himself and pitched it out into the little sunbright clearing before replying. 'Not unless he knows where we're goin', mister. It won't be north. Clems's too smart for that. An' they'll have to wait for daylight to track us. By then we'll be so far ahead no one'll catch us.'

Alan studied the man. He was ordinary in every way. One thing might have set him apart, his tied-down holster with its scooped-low cut-out holster. A lot of men with little more than instinct were perfectly coordinated, and that made professional gunmen. They lacked, among other things, a conscience, a noticeable degree of intelligence, and feelings. But none of those things were necessary to individuals who lived by violence and who would, according to a number of authorities, perish from violence.

The posseman arose, dusted his britches and went over where Deputy Comstock was leaning back with his hat tipped down. He wasn't sleeping, he was figuring. When the other man came up and leaned on his Winchester, Comstock looked up at him with eyes as cold as the lidless eyes of a rattler. 'He try to bribe you, did he?' Comstock asked and the other man shook his head.

'Nope. We just sort of talked. He said if we get Schilling, Dougherty an' his outfit will be after us.'

Comstock yawned. 'We knew that, didn't we?'

'I reckon. But you know, Clem, when I seen him whip out that big knife in Gardea's yard, I decided he was a man who'd never let up.'

Comstock straightened up, spat aside and re-set his hat. 'Fine. Let him keep comin'. We'll ambush the son of a bitch. Them greaser riders of his will scatter every which way when they see Dougherty go down

... You still got some of them dried apples in your saddlebag?'

As the posse-rider went to find his horse Comstock heaved up to his feet and went out where Alan was sitting. He hunkered down, eyed the opposite canyon wall and spoke in a gravelly voice. 'How much land does Dougherty own? I don't mean this gully, I mean good grass land.'

'Thirty-five thousand acres.'

Comstock swung his gaze to Alan Gardea. 'No one owns that much land. I've worked through Montana an' Wyoming where they got some big spreads. No one owns no thirty thousand acres. Hell, he'd go up over the line into Colorado.'

'And southward down into the southern desert country. West as far as my boundary and east farther than a man can ride in several days on a real sound horse.'

Comstock continued to gaze at the younger man. 'How many cattle does he run – an' don't tell me a million or some other darned lie.'

Alan did not know how many cattle the Dougherties ran. Years earlier he'd heard his father mention the figure of four thousand mammy cows, which was seed stock. He had not mentioned the bulls – one to forty cows – nor the big calves and steers. He watched Comstock pick up a twig and draw numbers in the dust, erase them and write down another set of numbers. This time he sat hunched, lost in thought as he gazed fixedly at the scratching. 'Hell,' he softly said. 'I been wastin' my time. Schilling ain't worth a fraction of what your uncle's worth.' Comstock tossed away the little stick. 'Tell you something, Mister Rancher, if he's got ten riders or thereabout, an' there ain't a bank in Nowhere – does he keep a lot of money for wages an' other things in his house?'

Alan truthfully did not know if his uncle kept a lot of money around. He replied to Comstock in a flat-toned voice. 'You got one chance in a hundred of getting away from there with Charley Schilling. If you do that it'll be a miracle. If you hang around searching for my uncle's cache, the odds against you getting clear will multiply to about a thousand to one.'

Comstock replied in a very quiet, menacing tone of voice. 'Well now, friend, there's a lot of ways to make a search real short an' real productive. Like usin' hostages.'

Alan did not like the big man's expression. 'How?' he asked, and got a straight-out answer. 'There'll be womenfolk over there. We'll shove their feet into a fire. You'd be surprised how well that works.'

Alan continued to regard the large man. 'With a badge on your shirt?'

Comstock snorted. 'Damned badge is no good down here, an' back up where I come from, badges can be found on some pretty big-moneyed folks.'

Alan thought of his handsome mother in this man's grasp. It was a chilling thought. 'The badge doesn't mean anything?'

Comstock wagged his shaggy head. 'Not down here, mister, an' not up where we come from – unless we want it to up there.' He grinned at Alan Gardea. 'Take your sheriff now. He's got a nice badge, an' he ain't got the gumption to pull a sick man out of bed.'

Alan sat gazing at the big man in stony silence until Comstock went back to his riders, was handed some dried apples and began to eat them.

The day was wearing along. It was now mid-afternoon, and as sure as the sun rose, John Bristow and the riders with him were prowling and searching.

By now there could be no doubt but that Alf and Alan Gardea had been caught.

But John was not prowling alone. He had watched a rider sashaying over the tracks they had left since leaving town and while he thought he knew who that distant horseman was, until the tracker was much closer he did not recognize him: Sheriff Burt Evans with a saddlegun peeping up over the neck of his saddle animal.

Bristow had a lot of time to think about what should be done: fade deeper into cover and hope Evans couldn't continue to track them, or go out and meet the lawman. John Bristow had little affection for lawmen, even ones like Burt Evans whom he had known a long time and respected.

The *vaquero* standing nearest to Bristow in the covert, spoke in Spanish. 'The lawman. He is reading our sign.'

Bristow grunted, his decision almost made for him, and walked down out of the underbrush into Burt Evans's sight.

The sheriff rode up, halted and leaned on his saddlehorn as he regarded the hard-faced older Gardea rangeboss. 'Well, where do we go from here?' he asked Bristow, whose reply was about his anxiety at both Alan and Alf Olmstead being gone for something like three hours.

Sheriff Evans nodded, straightened in the saddle and studied the flow of empty land. He said, 'You know where Ghost Canyon is, John?'

Bristow nodded.

'Well, look around you. There's no decent cover as far as you can see, unless it's yonder in the distance where sunlight is bouncin' off the tin roofs of Dougherty's outbuildings.' Evans looked down. 'Did

Alan ride toward the canyon?'

'Sort of in that direction, yes.'

'Any sign of other riders?'

'Yeah. Three riders ... Hell, they could be down in that canyon, Sheriff.'

Evans smiled slightly. 'You just had a good idea,' he said drily. 'I'll ride ahead. You gents can foller. But don't foller any tracks down into the *arroyo*, split up and ride on each side of it. An' be damned careful. If Comstock's down there he'll be watchin' the rims.'

As Sheriff Evans evened-up his reins he also said, 'If he's got Alan an' he sees us, he'll have a hostage to trade with. Or he may shoot him.'

Sheriff Evans rode on, did not look back and watched for the initial low place where the *arroyo* began, then ran deeper and wider in a north-easterly direction.

He stopped, twisted, saw Bristow and his riders approaching, and swung to the ground with an upheld hand. As the Gardea riders halted Burt Evans said, 'On second thought, gents, let's leave one man for a horse-holder and do the rest of it on foot ... And stay back from the edge.' He nodded in the direction of the slanting-away sun. 'We'll cast long shadows as we move. Keep far enough back so no shadows can fall into the *arroyo*.

The rangeboss nodded without comment. It probably did not enter his mind that Sheriff Evans had usurped his position as head Indian, and right now, if the idea had crossed John Bristow's mind he wouldn't have given it a second thought. He was a direct man not given to innuendos, false pride or an inability to relinquish control if whoever took charge had the same interest and meant to implement it.

They split up. Bristow took the east side and

remained back from the edge of the *arroyo* a fair distance, even though the lowering sun cast the shadows on the easterly side of the *arroyo* eastward, nowhere near the cliff-face above the *arroyo*.

Each man had a saddlegun. Sheriff Evans, on the west side of the *arroyo*, moved steadily but without haste. He kept sufficient distance so the slanting sun would not project shadows down where men would be watching for movement of any kind.

In the far distance a cloud of dust arose above a party of loping horsemen. Except for the dust they would not have been noticeable even though they were moving.

Sheriff Evans stopped to watch briefly, then led off on his northward hike again. If that was Dougherty and his riding crew they would be too distant to help, or hinder, the manhunt.

Evans had to force his thoughts off Charley Schilling among that large scattering of buildings slightly more eastward than northward in the middle distance. As he'd told Alan Gardea, he really didn't much care about the fate of the fugitive. In Burt Evans's book murder was murder and the worst kind was back-shooting. There could be mitigations from hell to heaven and as far as the sheriff on the west side of Ghost Canyon was concerned his oath required him to apprehend criminals. In his opinion the worst criminals were murderers.

He hadn't really pushed his search for Charley Schilling as zealously as he might have if the fugitive hadn't been in the custody of one of his best friends, but he would not let even that interfere when there was a showdown.

Right now, with the sun a coppery-red disc a few yards above a very distant upheaval of ancient hills, frozen for all time in their grotesque and tortured shapes, Burt Evans the lawman wanted Deputy Comstock, another lawman. The irony did not occur to him as he came to the place where a small clearing showed plainly trampled grass.

He went ahead alone, approaching the high bluff in a low crouch, and crawled the last few yards to a position just short of the drop-off where he could see down into the *arroyo*.

He did not see much: some trees, the sluggish creek, and tracks which did not appear to go any farther than that little clearing.

He lay a long time, and was eventually rewarded by hearing someone say something about dried apples. The words were clear but faint. It was enough.

He crawled back, got to his feet and with an upraised arm signalled John Bristow across the *arroyo* and some distance back from it. He wig-wagged his hat, saw Bristow and his companion halt. He wig-wagged more furiously. Bristow dismounted.

It seemed to the sheriff as though they were making their horses fast in the scrub brush. He turned back to find his own Gardea rider. They too left their animals tied and started very cautiously toward the same lip of land where Sheriff Evans had heard the man say something about dried apples.

Those distant horsemen had been making a bee-line toward the Dougherty yard. They were no longer in sight among the buildings, but their dust-banner continued to hang in the still air.

12 More Blood

What ensued was one of those things caused by accident. A rock about the size of a fist came loose up above and rattled down the side of the *arroyo*.

One of Comstock's riders sprang up. His companion, relaxed with his back to a tree looked up and around, but seemed to believe a tumbling stone in that earthen westerly bulwark was natural.

Comstock himself came back where his men were and strained to see upwards. Shadows were puddling down in the *arroyo*, nearby horses were dozing. The rock hadn't upset them.

The big bearded man hesitated. The rock might have worked loose by itself. The dozing horses hadn't heeded its fall and only one of his men was on his feet with his carbine.

Overhead, Burt Evans and his companion squirmed back from the rim. Burt swore under his breath. He was here to fight, but not to be stampeded into it. Maybe the damned rock had worked loose by itself, but if it had it had picked a damned poor time to do it.

Burt clearly heard Comstock growl at one of his riders to get a-horseback and go back up until he could see the flat country. He warned the posseman to be damned careful not to let himself be seen.

Comstock hunkered near the other posse-rider and waited until the man who had sprung up when the stone had fallen was picking his way back up through the trees and underbrush, then he loosened a little and spoke to his remaining rider.

'If anyone's up there it's got to be them damned Gardea riders.'

The relaxing man replied quietly. 'Look at that wall, Clem. There's rocks shot all through it. They been fallin' down in here for a hunnert years.'

'Maybe. But Gardea told me his riders would be along.'

That made his rider straighten up and scowl. After a moment of thought he said, 'Naw; they'd head for the Dougherty place.'

'Like hell they would. They'd follow the tracks, an' they lead down in here.'

The rider accepted that. 'All right. We'll catch them like we caught their boss and that other one.'

Comstock seemed to be placated by that remark. In fact he even smiled wolfishly at his rider. But he waited for his other man as his companion arose slowly and went prowling out through the trees where the horses were standing, and scanned the cliff-face. He saw nothing worth noting and started back, confident the rider who had been sent to scout would return shortly.

He didn't. He had picked his way quietly and carefully to the area where the canyon sloped upwards, left his horse tied and with a carbine in one hand, did the rest of his scouting on foot – and walked right into the gun-barrel of a grinning *vaquero* who put a finger to his lips for silence.

John Bristow came out of some underbrush, also with a gun in his fist, and softly said, 'You boys talk too much. We heard everything Comstock said. Now just let the Winchester drop. That's fine. Now the belt-gun.'

The posseman looked stonily at Bristow. 'You pull that trigger an' the noise'll carry a damned mile.'

John's hard looked softened into a small smile. 'Good. That'll bring Dougherty and his riders. Right now I'd sort of like that.'

The Wyoming gunman dropped his sixgun.

Bristow had a question for him. 'Who's he got down there with him?'

'Your boss, a lanky rider, himself an' another one of us.' Now the gunman smiled. 'You do anything at all, rangeboss, and Gardea will be shot first.'

John leathered his weapon and motioned for the captive to move farther from the canyon, back towards a thicket of thorn-bush. The grinning *vaquero* herded him along with an occasional prod in the back.

Where they stopped Bristow addressed the *vaquero*. 'Go way to hell out and around over where the sheriff is. He can see the west side of the clearing better'n we can. Tell him we caught one of the bastards an' for him to sneak up and see what he can make out where Comstock is.'

As the *vaquero* went after his horse John motioned for his prisoner to sit on the ground.

The posseman was dark-skinned and brown-eyed. His hair was black and badly needed shearing. Without a glance at Bristow he went to work manufacturing a cigarette. When he had lighted up he offered the sack and John shook his head. He chewed; he did not smoke.

The captive eyed Bristow shrewdly. John stood back a short distance returning the other man's gaze as he said, 'You're a damn fool. There's only Comstock and one other of you fellers left.'

'An' you shot two of us that are missing.'

Bristow shook his head. 'They're both at the Gardea place. One's got a hurt leg. Jess Coon. The other one's not hurt an' eats like a horse. Willard Bowman.'

The dark man studied Bristow through trickling smoke for a long moment before speaking again. 'You're lyin'. Clem Comstock don't know anything like or he'd act different.'

Bristow knew nothing about that, although if he'd reflected he would probably have come to the same conclusion that Alan Gardea had probably told the same story to Deputy Comstock. He shrugged, a Mexican characteristic he'd acquired without being conscious of it. 'Believe what you want,' he told the prisoner. 'What's your name?'

'Jack Bluestone.'

'In'ian?'

'A third.'

'Well, Jack Bluestone, you're lucky. You'n Bowman an' Coon might live through this ... Did you believe you could sneak in over yonder and make off with Charley Schilling?'

The dark man's gaze flipped away from John's face, went toward the slope where the *arroyo* began, and returned before he replied. 'Clem Comstock's been in tighter fixes than this one.'

'A man's luck don't last forever. If he tries to get Schilling, he'll never make it.' John gestured back across the *arroyo*. 'The sheriff's over there an' he ain't alone. He can see into them trees where you fellers was when that damned rock dropped.'

Jack Bluestone straightened slightly and raked the far rim with narrowed eyes. He saw no one, but he was beginning to wonder if Bristow did not lie. He smashed his smoke against the ground and said, 'Fact is, rangeboss, I ain't felt real easy since Schilling shot that feller who rode with us. An' after that face-down in Gardea's yard ... Who the hell were all them riders anyway?'

'The red-headed feller with the knife is Alan Gardea's uncle, that's his yard you fellers saw over yonder. That's where Schilling is.' Bristow squatted across from his prisoner. 'Comstock's goin' to get himself an' the feller with him killed as sure as we're settin' here. It's plain crazy for him to keep on tryin' to get Schilling.'

The 'breed smiled tightly at John Bristow. 'Try tellin' that to Clem Comstock, mister. He's never yet come back off a manhunt empty-handed.'

'You think he can succeed?'

The 'breed's dark gaze swung away, then back again before he answered. 'I know for a damned fact he'll try.'

Bristow wagged his head at the other man, fished for his tobacco plug, bit off a sliver and offered the plug, but the dark man shook his head. 'Tried it a couple of times an' was sicker'n a dog. Rangeboss ...?'

'Yeah.'

'Now what? We goin' to set out here forever?'

John was pocketing his plug when he answered. 'No. We're goin' to set here until someone does something, then I'm goin' to knock you over the head and get into it.'

'Why didn't you just ride to the Dougherty place an' bring them back with you?'

John shrugged again. 'I'm just the rangeboss. Alan Gardea makes the decisions ... most of the time ... you got a family up in Wyoming?'

'Not in Wyoming, in Montana.'

Bristow spat aside, stood up and went to retrieve

his prisoner's weapons. When he started back the 'breed said, 'You thought I'd duck into the brush, didn't you? Mister, you ain't goin' to shoot me in the back. Not this time anyway.'

Bristow cocked an eye at the sun, then across the *arroyo*. He saw nothing over there and the afternoon was wearing along. He faced his prisoner, and without warning two gunshots sent echoes in all directions. Jack Bluestone straightened up. John Bristow had placed one of those shots from down in the canyon, the other one from the cliff on the east side of the *arroyo*.

A man called loudly. 'Come out of the trees, Comstock!'

There was no reply, no sound at all for a long time. Not until someone across the *arroyo* tried ground-sluicing with a rapid-firing carbine. This time the echoes lasted longer before being swallowed up by distance.

The same voice called again. 'Comstock! There'll be a damned army of riders out here soon. Come out of the trees!'

Again there was no reply.

Jack Bluestone spoke into the returning silence. 'They got to go down in there to smoke him out.'

Bristow waited in silence. The stealth was over. Now the fighting would continue; he was more satisfied. Skulking had never appealed to him. He was a direct individual.

Time ran on. Jack Bluestone was listening intently when John Bristow said, 'You won't hear 'em goin' down in there,' and the 'breed answered curtly. 'I wasn't listenin' for them.' He did not elaborate but the implication was clear.

Bristow hooked the carbine in the crook of one arm

as he considered his prisoner. Bluestone saw the look and grimaced. But Bristow did not swing the carbine, he instead ordered the 'breed to get belly down with both hands in back, lashed the man's arms with Bluestone's belt, used both their bandanas to tie him tightly at the ankles, and as he started to arise he rolled the 'breed on to his back and gave him a warning. 'You make a sound – try yellin' a warning, I'll come back and bust your head like a rotten melon.'

The 'breed watched John Bristow head toward the sloping ground where the *arroyo* arose from its depths to meet the higher, flatter ground.

There were shadows down in the *arroyo* although the sun was still fairly high. John stopped twice because he thought he had heard something below, then went within a few yards of the rising land and knelt with his carbine. For whoever had survived down there, there was only one way out, back the way they had ridden down. There was another way but it was toward the Dougherty yard and neither Comstock nor his remaining posse-rider would go in that direction.

He heard something just over the upper rise of the *arroyo*. Across the way there was neither sound nor movement.

So abruptly it caught Bristow by surprise, a rider burst out of the *arroyo* riding in a belly-down run. His head was swinging from side to side. He saw the rangeboss as Bristow was raising his Winchester. The desperately fleeing man had a sixgun already up and swinging. He fired first, and missed. He ducked down the side of his horse as John fired. The bullet passed over the saddle and would have struck the rider if he'd been upright.

The horse, inspired to even greater effort by the gunfire, was straining ahead with each bound when his rider fired twice more as he hauled himself back upright. His second shot scored. Bristow went over backwards under impact, his trigger finger spasmodically tightening. His carbine was pointing upward when the gun fired.

The rider raced ahead half-twisted in the saddle. He saw the rangeboss fall and leathered his weapon in order to concentrate his full attention upon escaping.

Farther back a band of horsemen appeared on the land above the *arroyo*, saw the fleeing man and spurred in pursuit, but the escaping man was too far ahead, and the Dougherty riders had to come around to the west side of the *arroyo* to press their chase. One of them tried a long shot with a saddlegun. The distance was too great.

Two more horsemen appeared up out of the *arroyo* and Patrick Dougherty flung up an arm and yelled not to shoot. He had recognized his nephew.

Alan and Alf Olmstead stopped, sat watching the escaping horseman, and were waiting when the Dougherty riders came up.

Patrick Dougherty was slightly breathless when he called to his nephew. 'Was that Comstock, Alan?'

'Yes,' Gardea replied, bitterly watching the escaping man growing smaller in the southward distance with each passing moment.

Two riders loped around from the east side of the *arroyo* and joined the others watching the big bearded man getting clear.

Sheriff Evans said, 'That son of a bitch. I thought it was him. Someone was moving among the trees. He fired at us but missed by a country mile, likely didn't even see us to aim at. Both of us shot back at the same time. He was down there at the edge of the little clearing.'

Alan swung off, went over where his rangeboss was lying and looked pale as he rolled Bristow on to his back.

Dry ground was absorbing blood and Bristow's upper shirt-front was soaked with it. Patrick Dougherty came up, knelt, probed for the injury and said something in Spanish to a heavy-set man with a fierce up-curling grey moustache.

The wound was jagged where the slug had exited in back. In front there was a puckered hole already swelling and turning blue. The stocky *vaquero* came hurrying back with a bundle, which he handed to the man with the grey-streaked carroty hair.

With everyone watching, Patrick Dougherty snipped torn flesh away from the exit wound and sprinkled some grey powder, wiped blood away and sprinkled more of the grey powder until the bleeding lessened to a tiny trickle.

The front wound scarcely bled at all. Dougherty sprinkled more of the grey powder on it anyway, and handed the bundle to the stocky man with the up-curling moustache as he ordered in Spanish for a travois to be fashioned from dead oak limbs from the *arroyo* and a couple of the tightly-rolled single blankets behind nearly every cantle of his riders.

Dougherty met his nephew's gaze above the body of the wounded man. 'Damned near the same wound as Charley Schilling has.'

Alan looked down. There was blood everywhere and Bristow's face was grey. Unconsciousness was in this case a blessing, otherwise the pain would have been almost unbearable.

Sheriff Evans looked southward but the fleeing man was no longer in sight. He speculated on where he would go. The Mexican boundary line was farther south than Comstock could make on the horse he was riding, unless he spared the animal, and even then he might not make it.

It was waterless country down there, sparsely inhabited and genuinely hostile to men and animals alike.

They got Bristow on to the improvized travois and one of the men, the one who had been riding the horse the travois was fitted to, led his animal as the Dougherty riders started back to the ranch.

That stocky, dark *vaquero* with the impressive moustache remained behind with Alan, the sheriff and two Gardea riders. It was the dark man who heard the 'breed calling and went, gun in hand, hunting for him. Where they met the 'breed was looking straight up as the *vaquero* cocked his weapon.

Burt Evans called to him in Spanish. Very gradually the man with the fierce moustache lowered his weapon but did not ease the dog down until the others had come up and Alan knelt to free the posse-rider.

The Mexican *vaquero* looked stonily at the freed captive. '*Muera*,' he said coldly. May he die. Sheriff Evans told the stocky man to ease the hammer down and holster his weapon, which was done, but the look on the *vaquero*'s face did not change.

13 The *Alcalde*

John Bristow was more than Alan Gardea's range-boss; he was also his long-standing friend and companion, utterly loyal to the Gardeas.

Alan did not go to the main house where they carried Bristow, he collared the big *vaquero* named Juan Aguilar and took him to the barn. They saddled two fresh Dougherty horses and left the yard at a fast walk.

Alan explained everything to the big Mexican as they rode. By the time Aguilar had digested it all he was as anxious to find the bearded Wyoming deputy sheriff as Alan was.

The day was waning as they loped past *Cañon Fantasmas*, picked up Comstock's tracks and continued to lope down them for a half-hour before dropping to a steady walk for another half-hour.

Juan rode peering ahead as he asked about the captured 'breed, who had been taken to the Dougherty yard astride the horse he'd left just below the lip of the *arroyo*.

Alan could tell him little. John Bristow could have done a better job but he was out of it. Juan said, 'If John dies I'll kill him.'

Alan did not reply. That the 'breed had not shot John Bristow did not matter to people like Juan Aguilar; he had been 'one of them'. That was all that mattered.

Comstock's running horse dug in hard with his rear

hooves, leaving unmistakable imprints, even as the afternoon began to fade.

His pursuers knew the country and assumed – correctly – that Deputy Comstock did not.

Sheriff Evans had gone down into the canyon and found a dead posse-rider down there, whom he left where the man had fallen with a slug through his brisket. Later, he told the others; right at the time John Bristow was more important. Maybe in the morning someone could come back for the dead man.

Juan Aguilar knew the south country very well. He had at one time or another, for varying reasons, traversed every mile of it.

There were a few isolated hovels down there, about like the one old Augustino Madrigal lived in, commonly inhabited by other people who also raised goats, practically the only beast that could thrive on the kind of forage that existed the farther south they rode.

After sundown they passed the lights of Nowhere a mile out, still tracking Comstock, but on foot leading their animals.

The tracks became difficult to make out because now, Comstock, undoubtedly feeling safe, had dropped down to a walking gait, probably because he realized he had to favour the horse.

Alan also knew the southerly country. Gardea holdings went a considerable distance southward into the drier, less favourable country where Gardea cattle were pushed early each year in order to take advantage of the abundant grass that came as a result of springtime rains, and dried out very quickly when the rains stopped and desert heat arrived.

There were no towns, not even villages, until travellers – or fugitives – got almost to the border, then they were wretched little places inhabited since earliest times by lethargic, mostly dispirited people who had been born into hardship, expected nothing different, and continued to perpetuate the misery through generations of others who perhaps accepted their lot, through infusions of their mother's milk; but at any rate, they were for the most part deferential people, at times treacherous, at other times excitable and unpredictable, their heritage a mixture of wildly exuberant Anahuac, and Spanish practicality.

Anything was for sale in those wretched little villages, and nothing was safe from theft. As Juan Aguilar said as they approached a huddle of distant candle lights, 'If Comstock stops down here, and makes the mistake of resting, when he goes outside his horse and saddle will be gone.'

Alan too watched the weak lights up ahead. They were still a fair distance from the border. Without question the big man knew by now how valuable his horse was. If he was to continue to lead the pursuit he knew very well would be after him, he had to take very good care of his animal.

They approached the nearest hovel showing candle light, riding slowly and warily. A dog barked; the sound was taken up by other rat-tailed mongrels. Alan dismounted near the *jacal*, handed Juan his reins and was approaching the door when a short, burly, very dark *mestizo* stepped out with an old trap-door rifle held in both hands across his body.

He stopped stock-still when he saw the mounted man farther back and the other man walking toward him. He did not challenge them, perhaps because he had thought the barking dogs meant prowling coyotes, the bane of all sheep and goat people.

Alan addressed the *mestizo* in Spanish, asking where he and his companion could find feed and water for their horses and perhaps a little *cantina* with rooms for themselves.

The stocky man grounded his old rifle, looking from Alan to Juan and back. When he spoke he startled both the Gardea men.

'*Señores*, the village of Agua Prieta has maybe one or two visitors a year. We are a poor people with little worth taking from us. We avoid involvement in the Mexican troubles and we have no reason to expect *gringo* riders in the night ... There is a *cantina*, but no rooms. There is no place to sleep except in private homes. You can get water for your horses down there,' the stocky man gestured toward a dusty old plaza with a dug-well in the centre of it, where water was drawn by a rickety arrangement from which was suspended a wooden bucket.

The *peon* smiled at Alan. 'You can sleep out behind my house.There is a strong scent of goats.' The stocky man shrugged and continued to smile as he also said, 'As I said, *Patrón*, we are a very poor people.'

Neither Alan nor big Juan Aguilar had any trouble understanding the implication. Alan fished some coins from a pocket and extended his hand, but when the stocky man reached Alan pulled his hand back and asked a question.

'There has been another stranger, companion. A *gringo* with a great beard ...'

The *mestizo* looked steadily at Alan Gardea before replying. 'Strangers, especially *gringo* strangers, come here very rarely, *Patrón*. This man with the beard, there is a reward on him and you are lawmen in pursuit of him?'

Alan gazed at the shorter, thicker man for a

moment before saying, 'Fifty American dollars, friend. Is he here?'

Fifty US dollars was a fortune to the short man. He looked past at big Juan Aguilar, then back to Gardea as he said, '*Señores*, my name is Enrique Sosa. If I tell you where this *gringo* is, will I get the fifty dollars?'

Alan nodded and Juan Aguilar finally dismounted to hold both horses as he listened.

Enrique Sosa stood briefly in thought then held out his hand and Alan dropped the coins in it. Sosa looked at them in the weak light and closed his fingers around them tightly as he jutted his chin in a southerly direction.

'That house with the blue front. That is the residence of Fernando Paredes. He is our *alcalde*. He sees that laws are obeyed as well as being *mayór*.' Enrique Sosa lapsed into a long moment of silence before continuing. 'He is a man of temper. If he learns I told you where his guest is, he would kill me.'

Alan replied quietly. 'Your name will not be mentioned. Is the big *gringo* in his house?'

'Yes. And his horse was fed and watered in the stable behind the house ... *Señores*, remember, the *alcalde* is a powerful man ... when will I get the fifty *norteamericano* dollars?'

Alan drew a roll of greenbacks from a pocket and under the covetous eyes of Enrique Sosa, counted out fifty dollars and handed them to the burly man, along with an admonition. 'Go back inside. Go to bed. If you try to warn the *alcalde* we'll kill you. You understand?'

Enrique Sosa clutched the fortune in his free fist and looked reproachfully at Alan. '*Patrón*, I live by the law. I am a man of honour, you can ask anyone in Agua Prieta. Besides, I am very tired and sleep like a stone ... *Gracias, Patrón. Muchas gracias.*'

There were fewer lights showing as Alan and Juan Aguilar left the village riding west. A few dogs barked, which was inevitable, but since they barked at any foreign sound or scent, including those of nocturnal varmints in search of trash barrels, it was reasonably safe to ignore them.

Alan went out a half-mile, then turned back on a slack rein aiming for the rear of the house with the blue-painted front.

He and Juan Aguilar left their mounts out a short distance, approached the mud-wattle stable with its faggot corral, saw the horse watching them, and with no effort got a shank on the docile animal and led it back out where their animals were tied, and left it.

Clem Comstock was now on foot. There were no other horses in the faggot corral and while there undoubtedly were other horses in the village, Comstock might have trouble finding them, and even more trouble if he tried to steal one.

The *alcalde*'s house had a bolt-studded rear door made in the form of an arch. Whoever had put it there had been either ignorant or careless; the bolted hinges were on the outside.

Juan Aguilar got finger grips on both sides of the door and strained, rested and strained again. The door came up off its upturned bolts with scarcely a sound. Juan placed it gently against the back wall and showed white teeth in his grin at Alan.

Inside, the darkness was solid. Somewhere a man was snoring in the even cadence of a sound sleeper. They used that sound to penetrate from the rear of the house to an ajar door behind which was the snoring man.

Alan did not push the door inward, he gripped the latch and lifted, then very gently eased the door back without a sound.

The man in the bed was fat, blankets over his middle formed a mound which fell away above and below. Juan Aguilar went to a cane-bottomed chair, removed the gun hanging there by its shellbelt, and shoved it into the front of his trousers.

Alan went to the side of the bed. The snoring man was not Deputy Comstock. He motioned for Juan Aguilar to follow him and went soundlessly back into the darkness where he whispered, 'Watch that one. He must be the *alcalde*.'

Juan nodded and slipped back into the snoring man's room while Alan crossed a parlour with saints prominently displayed on every wall, down a narrow, very dark hallway, opened the first door he saw a fraction and peeked in. There was a narrow window in the south wall which allowed ghostly starlight to enter. A woman with masses of black hair was sleeping on her side.

He eased back and went to the next door, and this one squeaked despite his careful efforts to avoid a sound as he pushed it inward.

The sleeper in this room was on his back with a great profusion of whiskers over the topmost blanket. He pitched a little fretfully at a sound which penetrated his mind but relaxed again after a moment.

Alan slipped inside looking for Comstock's sixgun. It was on a small bedside table within arm's reach of the large man, shellbelt coiled so that the sixgun holster was on top. There was a carbine leaning nearby.

Alan moved over the hard-packed earthen floor and was leaning to reach for the holstered Colt when someone in another room sneezed violently.

Comstock's head turned. Alan saw the open eyes staring in startled disbelief as he lunged, got the weapon in his fist and stepped back.

Comstock's eyes followed Alan's every move but he did not move in the bed. Alan cocked the Wyoming lawman's gun and softly said, 'Get out of there, put your pants on ... *Now*!'

Comstock continued to lie staring for a moment, then threw back his blankets and eased up to the edge of the bed. His trousers were across the seat of a chair. He spoke as he leaned for them.

'What the hell do you think you're doing?'

'What do you think I'm doing?' Alan replied. 'I'm going to take you back to Nowhere and hand you over to Sheriff Evans. You think the law down here is a joke? You'll find out. Stand still! Put on your shirt – and don't think the *alcalde*'s going to help you. One of my riders is with him. If he awakens he'll get hit over the head ... Button it. Now your boots.'

This time Deputy Comstock moved very slowly. He picked up one boot and sat on the edge of the bed as he pulled it on. He reached for the second boot and in the poor light Alan did not see him reach inside it instead of hooking fingers through the strap atop the boot.

Comstock got the second boot on and stood up, one hand slightly folded as he faced Gardea and said, 'I give the *alcalde* twenty dollars to put someone out front to watch. Damned Messicans you can't rely on any of 'em.'

'We came by the back,' Alan told him. 'You are on foot, Deputy. Now walk out of here and don't yell or make unnecessary sound. I'll be behind you. Go out to the kitchen and out the back door.'

Comstock obeyed to the letter, head slightly

lowered as though in thought. When they were outside he spoke without looking around. 'How many riders are with you?'

'One. He's with the *alcalde*. Go around the corral and keep walking.'

Comstock obeyed. He cleared the faggot corral and walked ahead into the night for several yards, then stopped, turned and fired from a distance of about thirty feet with the little under-and-over derringer in his right hand. Alan was not hit but the big bullet had come close enough to make him wince.

Comstock was cocking the belly-gun for his second – and last – shot when someone bellowed inside the house, and Alan fired.

Comstock was knocked to his knees; a smaller man would have gone over backwards under the impact. Comstock raised his right hand for the next shot; his finger would not constrict and after a moment he fell forward on his face.

Dogs all over the village were barking and somewhere a woman screamed in Spanish for her husband to stay indoors.

Juan Aguilar was sitting on a chair when the *alcalde* jerked straight up in his bed. Juan wig-wagged with his cocked Colt and the *alcalde*'s eyes widened to their limit. Juan said, 'Get up, *Mayór*. Stand up from your bed.'

The *alcalde* obeyed but sluggishly. He did not even glance in the direction of his shellbelt and empty holster. He stared at big Juan Aguilar. 'Who are you?'

'A friend,' Juan replied sardonically. 'Like you, I am a man of the law.' Juan arose and gestured for the *alcalde* to walk ahead of him. Juan wanted a shield. He had no way of knowing who had survived the fight outside.

As they reached the kitchen the *alcalde* hesitated. Whoever was still alive out there would probably shoot him. If it was Comstock he would think the *alcalde* had sold him out. If it was someone else, a companion of the man behind him, he could also shoot him.

The *alcalde* said, 'Listen, companion. The big man forced me to let him rest in my house.'

Behind Juan Aguilar a female voice with all the belligerence of a shrew, exclaimed loudly. 'Yes, he held a gun on you, liar. You took twenty *gringo* dollars from him.'

Juan turned. The woman had streaked grey hair, a sharp nose, a slightly ferret-like face and she was furious as she clutched a robe and swore at her husband. 'I tried to tell you – he was being pursued or he wouldn't have arrived here with a staggering horse. But you would help him like you've helped others. For money. Oh you imbecile! You could have got us all killed.' The shrew snorted. 'Forced you to let him rest in our house! Sainted Mother, for thirty years I've listened to your lies and watched your perfidy. You there with the gun. Take him with you. Take him out of my sight!'

Juan herded the *alcalde* as far as the faggot corral and stopped. '*Patrón*?' he said softly, and got a reply from farther out. When they reached him Alan was standing beside the dead deputy examining the little big-bore under-and-over derringer Comstock had carried in his boot.

At sight of Gardea the *alcalde* stopped dead still. He looked from Gardea to the big sprawled corpse and began to shake although, while it was late, it was not a cold night.

He said, '*Señor*, he forced me to hide him. What could I do?'

Alan tossed the little gun to Juan Aguilar and regarded the fat man. He said in English, 'You're a liar. I heard the woman screaming back there. You hid him for money. You've probably done a good business doing that with other fugitives. I think we'll take you back up north with us. If the law up there isn't interested maybe the army will be.'

'*Señor*,' groaned the fat man. 'Listen to me. We are very near the border. Everyone raids us, *guerrileros*, brigands, outlaws of the north, even *rurales* full of mescal.' The *alcalde* wrung his hands. 'We exist down here by bowing to whichever raider enters our village. Only the Indians did we fight because they would have killed us anyway. When this bearded man came to me yesterday on his worn-out horse, I took pity …'

'Twenty dollars worth of pity,' Alan interrupted to say. '*Alcalde*, we should shoot you.' Alan nodded toward the dead Wyoming lawman. 'He would have killed us and you know it.'

'For the love of God,' bleated the fat man.

Alan jerked his head. 'Juan, bring in the horses. All three of them. *Alcalde*, you help us hoist this carrion on a horse and tie him. It's a long ride where we came from down here. It will be an even longer ride back burdened with that man.'

The fat man bobbed his head. 'Of course, *Patrón*. I will help in any way I can.'

When Juan Aguilar returned the fat man did, indeed, grunt and groan as the three of them got Comstock belly down across his saddle, and helped tie him. When Juan and Alan Gardea mounted and Juan took the reins of the led-horse, Juan said, '*Alcalde*, if I ever have to hunt down another one you have hidden for money –'

'*Patrón*! On my sacred honour. Never will I help

another one. Never!'

Alan led off up through Agua Prieta's main roadway with a paling sky increasing visibility. As he and Juan Aguilar rode past the farthest house, the first *jacal* they had reached, a stocky *peon* was out front with a dumpy dark woman.

Alan looked from an expressionless face at Enrique Sosa, and winked. The *mestizo* winked back. Neither man spoke nor smiled as Alan, Juan, and their grisly burden passed out of Agua Prieta on their way back to Nowhere.

14 *Vaya Con Dios*

Sheriff Evans was having his second cup of black java when Alan and Juan Aguilar walked in, tired-looking and rumpled. Both had a dark shadowing of beard. Evans stared at them, then wordlessly filled two additional cups from the pot atop his little office stove, handed a cup to each man and went to sit at his desk as he said, 'Well ...?'

Juan jerked his head. 'He's belly-down on his horse out front.'

Burt Evans scowled. 'In broad daylight, for Chris'sake, with the whole town to see him?'

Alan nodded and tasted the hot coffee. It was strong enough to be used as embalming fluid. 'We caught up with him at a village called Agua Prieta.'

Evans nodded, he knew the place.

'We were going to bring him back to you alive, but he had a belly-gun in his boot. He fired and missed. I fired and didn't miss.'

Burt arose to look out of his single front wall window with the bars across it. People were crowding together across the roadway muttering among themselves. The sun was high, visibility was excellent from one end of Nowhere to the other end. Burt groaned and returned to his chair. 'Why didn't you tie up in the damned alley?'

Alan smiled tiredly. 'We'll take him around there if you wish.'

'No. Leave the bastard where he is. Everyone in town's seen him by now.'

Alan put the cup aside. 'How is John?'

Evans leaned with both hands clasped atop his desk. 'He was lookin' better when I brought that 'breed back an' locked him up. He wasn't conscious; he seemed to drift in and out, but your mother stopped the bleeding and patched him up. He didn't lose as much blood as Schilling did.' Burt grimaced. 'Neither one of 'em'll go to any fandango dances for a while. What am I supposed to do with Comstock?'

Alan shrugged. 'Bury him. Keep all his personal stuff to be carried back to Wyoming by the two posse-riders I've got at the ranch, and the 'breed, if you want to free him before a circuit-riding judge gets down here.'

Sheriff Evans threw up both hands. 'All right. You send them two you got at the ranch to me here in town an' I'll send the three of them home with Comstock's goods ... Alan, I talked to Charley Schilling – with your mother an' that big *mestizo* woman – listening and glaring.'

'What did he say?'

'Well, he told me he'd already told you the whole story, but he repeated it for me.'

'Did you arrest him?'

'Well … no. He can't go anywhere for a couple of months anyway.'

Alan considered the cup, raised it and drained it, made a grimace as he arose, and said, 'Burt, that's the worst damned coffee I ever tasted. *Vaminos*, Juan.'

He and Juan Aguilar rode up the main thoroughfare of Nowhere looking straight ahead. People watched them pass in silence.

When they were clear of town they left the stage road and loped in the direction of the Dougherty yard. As they passed *Cañon Fantasmas* two Dougherty *vaqueros* emerged leading a horse with a dead man tied across it. They waved, Alan and Juan waved back and continued to lope until they were close enough to the Dougherty yard to walk their horses the remaining distance.

Juan rubbed a scratchy jaw as he spoke. '*Patrón*, I hope what the sheriff said about John is right. Because if it isn't, I'm going to quit you and trail those other three until we're in open country, and kill each one of them.'

Alan said nothing. For one thing, he had begun to hope after listening to Burt Evans. For another thing if his rangeboss died, Juan Aguilar would not ride alone.

Before they entered the yard watchers from half-a-dozen places had passed word of their coming. Alan's uncle met them down at the barn where an old *vaquero* took their horses to be cared for, and clucked as he led the horses away; they were weary and as tucked up as snow birds.

Patrick Dougherty asked no questions but raised his eyebrows after Alan and Juan had dismounted. Other Dougherty riders were hovering. One of them called a greeting to Juan Aguilar in Spanish. The big *vaquero* raised a hand and made a throat-cutting sign across his neck. He said nothing and the watching people nodded with both understanding and approval.

Dougherty looked from Juan to Alan. 'You caught him?'

'And killed him,' Alan replied. 'We hauled the carcass back and left it tied in front of the jailhouse for Burt to take care of.'

'Come with me,' the older man said. 'Both of you look like somethin' the cat dragged in.'

They followed him to the main house where scowling Maria Escobar met them, hands crossed primly across her middle. She told Juan Aguilar to follow her and led off in the direction of the big Dougherty kitchen.

Before Alan's uncle took him to the room occupied by Charley Schilling, he said, 'There's a little problem, Alan.'

Gardea nodded woodenly. He had known for some time about the problem his uncle was endeavouring to be tactful about. 'He's one year older than I am, *tio*.'

Dougherty, older and more experienced, smiled slightly. 'Yes, but your mother is a very handsome woman.'

'Of fifty, *tio*.'

Dougherty gave it up. 'Come along,' he said, and went down to the room where Charley Schilling and Dorotea Gardea were quietly talking. She arose at sight of her son, and said, 'Thank God. What happened?'

Alan saw Charley Schilling watching him and shrugged. 'We found him. it was a dark night. He had a belly-gun and shot at me with it …'

'And?'

'And I shot him. We brought him back and left his carcass with Burt Evans.'

Dorotea Gardea's expression softened. As she walked toward the door she stopped, kissed her son's beard-stubbled cheek and said, 'I'll get you something to eat.'

For a long time after her departure the three men eyed one another in silence, then Patrick also left the room.

Alan sat on the little chair his mother had used and blew out a ragged big breath. Charley Schilling said, 'Hard trail?'

Alan nodded.

'You talked to Sheriff Evans in town?'

'Yes. He thinks you'll be bedridden for a month or so.'

Schilling smiled. 'I got up yesterday. Your mother helped me walk around. It won't be a month, Alan.'

Gardea shoved his hat back, got more comfortable on the chair and eyed the man in the bed. His colouring was good, his eyes were clear, he spoke easily and even smiled a little. Maybe – if Burt had spoken to him yesterday, and had seen how recovered he looked, he might have said a month as a signal to Alan that Schilling could still leave the country. For a fact, and Alan was well aware of it, Burt Evans hadn't liked what the law required him to do from the first time he and Alan had talked. Maybe the law in New Mexico Territory *was* different, but Alan doubted it; men were men no matter where they lived.

'Alan, you're tired.'

There was no question of that. Tired and hungry. But he ignored the statement and said, 'Charley, do you know how old my mother is?'

'Fifty.'

'And you're one year older than I am.'

Schilling did not reply for a long moment. His eyes did not leave Alan's face when he finally did speak. 'She is a beautiful woman. Kind and generous and ...'

'Yes? And?'

'And we talked. She would be very easy to fall in love with. Maybe to you she's your mother. To me, she is something I don't think I'll ever meet again.'

Alan sat watching Charley Schilling.

Charley looked strained as he continued speaking. 'Hell, why I wanted her to help me walk, get a little exercise. God knows I don't want to leave.'

'Have you told her you cared for her?'

'I told her how grateful I am, what a wonderful person she is ... Yes, I care for her.'

'Have you told her that?'

'No. I wish to hell you were in my boots for a while. I'll leave as soon as I can. In the night, most likely. I hate what that'll do to her, but if I try to drag it out, in the end it'll still have to be same. Do you understand?'

Alan did not reply.

Charley Schilling's face was sweat-shiny, his gaze was very troubled. 'I've thought about it over and over. The answer is always the same. Maybe a person can give away ten or fifteen years, and it could work. But not the number of years that separate us. Alan, this is worse than being shot.'

Gardea stood up, went to a side table, filled glasses with red wine and handed one glass to Charley Schilling and returned to the chair with the other glass.

They sipped wine in silence. Maria Escobar came unsmiling to the doorway. 'There is a meal awaiting you in the kitchen,' she said in Spanish, shot Charley

Schilling a hard glare and walked back the way she had come.

Alan finished the wine and began to feel much less tired. He stood up looking at Charley Schilling.

'She'll recover,' he said quietly. 'She told me at my father's funeral that her world went into the grave with him. That was a long time ago. She wouldn't say that now. But, yes, she'll have another heartache. I don't know much about women, Charley, but it seems to me every real heartache they get in life is caused by men.'

Alan went out to the big kitchen where Juan Aguilar had just finished a meal the size of which had two Dougherty *mestizos* and Maria Escobar eyeing him in awe.

While Alan was eating, the hefty dark woman shooed the other females out of the kitchen and sat down opposite Alan, watched him eat for a while, then spoke quietly. 'Juan Aguilar is a horse.'

Alan nodded without pausing at his meal except to say, 'He's also a good man to ride with, Maria.'

The dark woman looked at the door Juan Aguilar had used to leave the kitchen and return to the yard. She spoke again in the same soft tone of voice on an entirely different topic.

'Your mother ... *niño*, a healthy woman living alone is ...'

Alan pushed the empty place away. 'Maria, I'm not blind.'

Maria Escobar seemed enormously relieved. She even smiled. 'I don't know the word in English. In Spanish it is –'

'In English, Maria, it is – vulnerable.'

Maria nodded. 'About the same, eh? He is very nice to her.'

Alan sipped coffee as he waited.

'He is a handsome man, *niño*. Lonely women are – what did you call it?'

'Vulnerable.'

'Yes. I've watched – have seen it coming since he came to the house. *Niño*, I am a servant.'

'You've always been more than that, Maria.'

The dark woman blinked, looked quickly away, cleared her throat and spoke again. 'I love your mother. I am afraid of what will happen.'

Alan arose from the table as he replied. 'Time will pass, Maria.'

'What does that mean?'

'She'll have pain for a while, but time will pass.'

Maria Escobar's eyes widened. 'He ... they won't get married?'

'No. Believe me.' He did not tell her about his conversation with Charley Schilling. He kissed her cheek and went out to the yard, found Alf Olmstead and took him on the long ride back to the Gardea home-place. There, he had the Wyoming manhunters brought out, put on horses, and sent on their way toward Nowhere. He did not tell them that Deputy Comstock was dead. Burt Evans could do that.

Two Gardea *vaqueros* left the yard with the prisoners. The ride would be hard on Jess Coon, but he would survive it. The last thing Willard Bowman said to Alan, out front of the barn, was: '*Patrón* – I picked that up. *Patrón*, I'd like to come back some day.'

'You'll be welcome,' Alan replied and they shook hands.

Augustino Madrigal came up to say he would have to go home no matter how many *matadors*, killers, were out there, otherwise the coyotes would kill all his livestock.

Alan helped the old man bring in his *burro* to be saddled. The *burro*, with considerable time to discover the difference between scrub brush and sweet grass hay, was barn-sour. He did not want to leave, and when Augustino hit him the *burro* bucked the old man off. Watchers around the yard, including the old *vaquero* whose *jacal* Madrigal had shared, laughed, and Alan caught the mule, helped Augustino back on him, and the mule responded finally, evidently very reluctant, but he hiked along anyway.

Alan left Alf Olmstead at the ranch as straw-boss and got back to the Dougherty place after dark. He and his uncle ate a late supper then went out to the veranda with cups of wine to talk.

Maybe it was having a big meal then wine, but Alan fell asleep in his chair. His uncle roused him, led him to a spare bedroom and left him sprawled across the bed fully clothed.

Sheriff Evans rode out four days later to tell Alan that Comstock's surviving posse-riders had been stunned at the death of the man who had led them down into New Mexico.

Burt had given them Comstock's personal effects, released the 'breed and watched them head north back toward the country they had come from.

Sheriff Evans did not visit Charley Schilling. He had his own reasons for not doing this, but he and Alan talked a long while in tree-shade behind Alan's uncle's big old barn, and when the sheriff finally left the yard for his ride back to Nowhere, Alan watched him leave wearing a hint of a smile. Burt Evans had told Alan again, that Charley Schilling would be at least another month on his back. Perhaps to get his subtle point across, he had repeated it twice.

They had a private secret.

Alan visited John Bristow, whose toughness hastened his recovery, and when he carped about all the time they'd wasted when they should have been working the cattle, Alan told him he'd left Alf Olmstead at home to oversee things until the range-boss could resume his duties, and John nodded about that. Alf was Bristow's *segundo*, his straw-boss. Alf would make another gather and start working the cattle through at the marking ground.

When Bristow was satisfied about the work getting done, he said, 'How's Charley Schilling?'

Alan shrugged. 'He's improving but it will be a long while,' and the rangeboss nodded about that too. It wasn't the first lie Alan had ever told his rangeboss, but it was the first lie since he'd been much younger.

Alan bathed out behind the main house at the small building with its own hand-pump for that purpose, shaved and put on clean clothes, provided by Maria Escobar, then took his mother for a walk in the dwindling daylight while it was still warm.

Dorotea Gardea mentioned Charley Schilling. Her son listened, assured her that they could now all return to the Gardea yard. He told her they would borrow one of her brother's wagons, fill it with blankets and straw for Charley Schilling, and leave in a day or two.

She seemed pleased about that.

They left the Dougherty yard three days later with Dorotea on the wagon seat beside the *vaquero* who drove. She turned often and Charley smiled at her, wistfully, but she saw only the smile.

They had been back home seven days when Charley awakened Alan in the small hours of the night, handed him an envelope, thanked him for all he'd done, and crossed to the silent barn to fetch in his horse and saddle it.

Alan was on the patio when Charley rode out. He turned once toward the main-house before lining his horse out – not southward toward Mexico, but westerly. Many miles in that direction was California, where from what all Charley had heard the last few years, there was a rich gold strike. There, in all the excitement, Charley Schilling would be able to lose himself. If Wyoming law continued its search, which both Alan and Charley thought unlikely, he would move again, but neither the man fading in the darkness west of the Gardea yard, nor the man who watched him leave, were occupied with thoughts about that.

They thought in very different ways about Alan's mother. In the morning she would know, and by then Charley would be well on his way and also by then Alan would give her the letter.